Such A Long Night

LATRICE WILLIAMS

DEDICATED TO HEALING PEOPLE

Pray, Seek God and Go to Therapy! You are no less saved if you seek counsel and help from a medically trained professional! You NEED someone to talk to!

ACKNOWLEDGMENTS & SPECIAL THANKS:

To My Lord and Savior, Jesus Christ – I am nothing without You. I could not accomplish anything without You. Thank You for looking beyond my fault and continuing to see what You said before time.

To My children, the apple of my eye – You're grown and making your own life choices now but I'm grateful to share in this phase of your life. I pray that God will forever be the center and focus of your life and that you'll allow Him to guide you into His destiny and purpose for your life.

To My Family, Covenant Family and Friends – Thank you for continuing to support what God is doing through me and the ministries He has called me to. It's an honor to serve you. I am humbled that you continue to buy my books and glean from them. May God continually bless the seeds you've sown through your support and purchases.

OTHER PUBLISHED EBOOKS

Life's Experience
Hurt To Healing
Articles of Encouragement
Mediations, Heart, Mind & Soul
The Destiny Journal

<<<----->>>

CONTACT INFO
Email:
latricespeaks@latricewilliams.com

Main Website:
http://www.latricewilliams.com/

Facebook:
www.facebook.com/TheDestinyDriver/

Twitter:
https://www.twitter.com/LWDestinyDriver

Instagram:
www.instagram.com/thedestinydriver/

CHAPTER ONE

My thoughts were scattered! They were everywhere. I desired to do so much but I really couldn't decide where to start. I had so many unfulfilled dreams despite the many successes God had given me. I found myself quoting Proverbs 13:12 - "Hope deferred makes the heart sick but a longing fulfilled is a tree of life." I constantly mulled over my deferred hopes asking God when were my longings, my dreams - going to be fulfilled? I went from asking God _when_ to asking _if_ they would ever happen at all. I became hopeless while trying to bring hope to so many others.

I'll never forget the day that I was beyond frustrated and very despondent. My office was ice cold and I was wrapped up like an eskimo. Even with my long sweater on, I was still shivering. I sat in a huge office with no windows, yet there was no heat. Although the problem was temporary, the circumstance seemed to be magnified at the moment. What was worst, was the fact that my heart and life seemed to mirror my cold office space. I had such a huge heart to help others, to see them thrive and to reach their full potential in Christ but I felt there was no window for me. No warmth for my soul. I literally felt cold on the inside. Even dark at times.

It's amazing because when I was around others, they never saw it. Or let's just say, if they saw it, they didn't _see_ it.

On that particular day, I was in the hallway attending to my staff. As usual, I was making sure they had what they needed to complete some accounts they were working on. I was jovial, smiling, joking with them and no one was the wiser. Not my staff, not my management team. No one. Literally, as soon as I walked back into my icebox, the smile dropped. My shoulders slumped, and I breathed a deep sigh of heaviness – all before I got back to my desk that was only 10 feet at the most, from the door.

Sadly, this was a more accurate picture of my true state of mind. Distant. Heavy. And clouded by sadness.

I sat at my desk and attempted to get myself together. "Okay Lord, what can I do today?" I figured there had to be some way for me to get out of that blah place and actually make some progress.

Still, nothing came to me, but I knew there was so much to do. Why couldn't I just do something? Anything to be productive. I sat there with countless thoughts, ideas and more, running rampant through my mind but nothing actually came together.

It bothered me that I could get it together quickly when it was time to make it happen for others. I had no problem organizing events, compiling souvenir booklets, overseeing budgets, and producing in excellence for the visions of others. But in that moment, I couldn't find my wits about myself *for* myself.

Nobody would have believed that I was literally suffering in silence while I served everyone else.

Leaning forward on my desk, my hands covered my face. I blew out another long, deep, defeated sigh.

How in the world could I get somebody else's book project in perfect order and almost ready for publishing, yet I couldn't seem to get the words on the paper for my own book? I was at such a lost with this newest project, yet I could not shake the unction that I had to write it. I knew that the very thing I had dealt with and often still contended with was what someone else needed to read about.

The long nights which lasted for days and weeks and months. The highs and the lows. The ups and the downs.

Suffering in silence but continuing to serve others.

I knew this new book was necessary because in my heart I felt, it just couldn't have been – only me.

I sighed again and listened intently for a few quiet minutes to the music playing in the background. Music always seemed to help calm my mind. Today, that wasn't the case. I took several deep breaths, did some neck stretches and pressed Control-Alt- Delete on my keyboard.

I decided that I was going to lunch.

Alone.

It was not a day to rally with the staff. That day, I just needed to get away.

I thought that if I walked away – literally - for a break and came back, maybe I'd feel more in control. Just maybe I'd be able to organize my thoughts enough to get started and produce something.

Really? Produce something? How is it that I actually had this thought about myself?

The truth is, I'd overcome so much and made great strides after such a devastating loss of my marriage, home and seemingly my ministry. With God's help, I bounced back! I fought through what was intended to destroy me.

I successfully held my yearly conference for four years. I published two more books and even started a business. So far, I seemed to have overcome depression, lies, lack of support and more losses than one could count.

But in that moment, I felt like there was more to do and I had less than zero enthusiasm and no drive to make it happen.

Burn out? Maybe. Depression? Likely. I didn't have a name for it at that moment, but what I knew, was that it was time for a break.

Finally, I pushed away from my desk. I pulled my Rosetti purse and keys out of the drawer and attempted to push it all out of my mind. At least for an hour.

I quickly locked my office door and headed to the elevator. There always seemed to be someone looking for me or needing something in this building. I intentionally dropped my head. I didn't want to make eye contact with anyone. I didn't want to stop my hot pursuit of fresh air and room to breathe.

The closer I got to the elevator - my steps quickened. I rounded the corner, and anxiously pressed the elevator button. More like pounded it. I was more than relieved that the doors opened immediately. I think I may have been holding my breath for those few seconds that I waited.

"I'm almost there," I said out loud to myself. "Lord, please just let me get out the building before anyone asks for anything."

On the short ride down the elevator, my mind went back to an event that I attended that just may have put me in this seemingly downward tailspin.

I anxiously tapped my hand on my thigh wanting this short ride, that seemed to last an eternity, to hurry up and be over. I just needed to get to the first floor.

CHAPTER TWO

The bell dinged; semi pulling me out of my thoughts. As soon as the door cracked open, I darted out and quickly headed to the hallway on the right side of the building. It was sure to be quiet and provide a quick way out. I'm sure I was almost running. Almost as fast as the thoughts in my mind.

I burst out the dockside door, looking quickly to the left and the right.

Finally! I breathed in a deep sigh of relief.

My feet seemed to move even faster as I hurriedly walked further away from the building. Making it to the street, I turned left and walked out of the parking lot onto the sidewalk.

I was really looking for an escape and not just from the building.

I thought that if I walked for lunch, maybe I'd be able to shake my growing level of anxiety.

As I walked toward the nearby shopping plaza, my racing thoughts returned. I mulled over the entrepreneur networking event that I had recently attended, among other things that were plaguing me most days. And nights!

Lord, please help me understand how I got here - again. I went to that event hoping to get informed and even inspired. Instead - I left discouraged.

God, I feel horrible. I'm wearing the same clothes over and over again; I'm exhausted with my whole life! What has happened to me? I feel like nothing! Who did I think I was? To think I could actually run a business? Or lead a church again for that matter? Nobody wanted to pay me for anything or support me, with my non-degree having self… Well, I actually have an Honorary Doctorate of Theology. Don't get me started on that. I never celebrated that prestigious moment for real. I was just over it with the people who laughed and attempted to shame me. God, what is wrong with people? Humph! But some of those same people sure love my help and advice when it's free! They love my oil when they are going through and need someone to intercede. Ugh! I don't know what I was thinking. I guess I've always had big dreams. Oh well.

The more these overwhelmingly negative thoughts came, the lower my shoulders sagged. I was maneuvering my walk through blurred vision. Tears welled up in my eyes.

Tears that I'd held in for so long.

Even at that moment as I walked alone, I still refused to let them fall. A veil of heaviness seemed to shroud about me as I recalled the fact that none of my big dreams had ever materialized. Not even the promise that God had given me in His Word had shown up.

Despondently laughing to myself, I thought - *It's funny, from a young age, I always dreamed of being on big stages. HA!* I sarcastically laughed out loud remembering how I'd always wanted to sing with Patti LaBelle and Yolanda Adams. *Humph, that must have just been a dream or wish or whatever,* I lamented as I wiped the corners of my eyes. The tears may have formed but I still wasn't ready for them to fall just yet.

CHAPTER THREE

I made it to one of my favorite places to have lunch alone. I actually said - *out loud* - to myself – "girl, you are something else."

I could not have been the same woman who was just almost in tears. I was standing at the hostess desk of Bre's- a quaint little bistro that I frequented often, with not a tear in sight.

"Hi, Ms. Jackson, it's good to see you today." I was greeted by Latrell, one of the best hostesses at the restaurant. "Would you like your regular table by the window today? It's open."

I smiled big! I'm told that my smile is outright contagious. Except for the fact that most days, it didn't reach my eyes. In my mind, most people didn't notice anyway.

"Well hey, Latrell!" I responded, opening my arms to hug her. "It's good to see you too! I'd love that table. Thank you very much."

"You're welcome! Follow me right this way."

I liked this bright young lady and always tried to encourage her when I went to Bre's. Today was no different.

I followed her to the table, asking the usual question. "Latrell, how is school going?"

"Although I'm looking forward to my upcoming break - it's going well," Latrell said through her wide smile as we reached my table.

"That is good to hear. Don't forget what I told you last time." I dropped my purse in one chair and took the seat next to the window. I love window seats in restaurants and on planes.

"Oh yes ma'am, I will not forget that prophetic word. I wrote it in my journal, and I've been praying over it just like you said. As a matter of fact, some of what you said has already happened." Latrell's voice was about an octave higher as she excitedly spoke of the last time we saw each other.

"Glory to God!" I waved my right hand to God. I felt myself smile genuinely for a change. It always did my heart good when testimonies came back to me that God had fulfilled His words.

"Yes ma'am, glory to God! I really thank you for all that you've poured into me. You don't know how much it has helped me to stay on track and not give up. But I won't take up your lunch time anymore. Someone will be over to take your order soon."

"You're very welcome, Latrell. Thank you so much!"

"Enjoy your lunch," she said as she turned to make her way back to her post at the hostess desk. She smiled as she walked away, but in the mirrors ahead of her, I could see the puzzled look on her face. *Lord, I wonder did she pick up what I'm really feeling?* Sitting at the table, I looked out the window at

the traffic breezing by as I waited for my waiter to come over. *Lord, thank You that You keep making good on Your word. I am grateful for that,* I prayed silently. Once again, I sighed deeply. I was still battling the heaviness that I carried in. I may have worn a mask on the outside but inside, there was no hiding from it.

My thoughts were interrupted by a brown haired, grey eyed slender waitress that I'd never met before.

CHAPTER FOUR

"Hello ma'am. My name is Layla. I'll be serving you today. May I get you some water or another drink to start?"

Before I could answer, immediately I saw what looked like a mirror image of myself. Not in the physical description. It was in Layla's smile. It was present, just not in her eyes. I saw a deep-seated sadness that rocked me to the core. I saw an emptiness that I knew I could not ignore.

I couldn't ignore it because I didn't want her to live like I was living.

That was not her destiny! (Side note- WOW- isn't it amazing that we can go hard for other's destiny. Sometimes, harder than we do our own.)

What I was dealing with and had been through would not be in vain. I just had to wait until the right time to speak on it.

"Hello, Layla. I'm Maiya Jackson. And yes, I'll take water with lemon and sweet tea also."

"Yes ma'am, I'll get that for you and then take your order if you're ready."

"Thank you."

I watched her retreat quickly and saw the slight slump in her shoulders, further telling me that what I discerned was accurate. She was such a beautiful young lady with such a sad disposition.

I dropped my head and prayed quietly. *"Lord, You know where I am today, and You know that I have absolutely nothing to give to this baby unless You give it. So, if it's meant for me to say anything, You say it. You see her, and You knew we'd both be here today. Don't let me speak from my place of "knowing" unless You've graced me to do so. Comfort her even now, Lord. In Jesus name. Amen."*

As I lifted my head, I quickly dabbed the corners of my eyes. Layla was walking back to the table with my drinks. I didn't have time for tears.

"Here are your drinks, Ms. Jackson." She sat both purple-tinted glasses on the table along with the engraved coasters. "What would you like to order today?"

"I'll have the chicken and shrimp alfredo lunch special, with extra sauce please."

"Yes ma'am, will that be all?"

"Yes, I believe so. Thank you."

"You're welcome, I'll put this order in for you right now."

Layla walked away quicker than before this time. *"Lord, I hope I didn't unnerve the young lady."*

I knew that sometimes I could be intense without trying. And I was probably looking at the baby right hard. I shook my head and chuckled at myself. *"Well, Lord, if there is something to be done here today, let's do it."*

It was about 15 minutes before my food arrived at the table along with a teary eyed and clearly shaken Layla. *"Oh, Lord, here we go."*

"Here is your food, Ms. Jackson. I hope that everything is to your liking."

I liked this young lady already. She was a tough cookie and professional too. Whatever was trying to rattle or undo her - she was holding her own. Her hands were trembling, but she was holding her head high and holding back the obvious tears I saw in the corners of her eyes. I couldn't help but smile.

She reminded me of myself so much. Both good and bad.

"Thank you very much, Layla."

As Layla placed the bowl in front of me, I placed my hand on top of hers and asked her to sit.

"No ma'am, I really can't." Layla was adamant that it was against policy. She anxiously looked around continuing to refuse the seat I offered her.

What Layla didn't know was that I was what some would call a VIP guest. I had a great relationship with my niece Bre"- the owner. I knew that if she came out and saw Layla sitting - it was at my invitation. I assured her that it would be fine.

"Sit. Let's chat. I promise you, Bre" won't mind. But just for good measure, I'll text her and let her know that I've accosted you."

As I pulled out my phone to send that text, Layla apprehensively took a seat on the very edge of the chair across from me. She nervously wrung her fingers together and every so often looked around the room. I knew that she didn't want to get in trouble for breaking the policy.

Tucking my phone back in my purse, I smiled at Layla. I reached across the table and stilled her anxious hands. "It's going to be okay."

Tears instantly ran down both sides of Layla's face. A look of relief washed over her. She quickly wiped her tears away.

"Thank you." Her words were barely audible. "How do you know?" she asked.

"Know what?" I responded. I could be so nonchalant sometimes.

"That it's going to be okay. You don't even know what's wrong."

Instantly, I knew God was about to require another level of transparency from me. I wasn't even sure in that moment if I was able to do it.

I withdrew my hand, looked at the young lady, took a deep breath and said, "We're two of a kind."

Although Layla looked puzzled, she didn't say anything. She just listened.

I continued speaking. "I see your smile, but it doesn't reach your eyes. You do well when it comes to serving others - but you're wondering will your chance ever come? You have big dreams and all of them seemed to have failed. Now you're asking God, why did I ever think that it could be? You're one who serves well yet suffers - in silence."

Layla's mouth opened but words never came out. She snapped her mouth shut but still looked at me in amazement. Her nervous anxiety increased. The look on her face said – *This cannot be real.*

I could be wrong, but I probably would have thought the same thing. Especially the way I went in right quick. Sometimes, I wished I could just turn it off! On the other hand, I'd temporarily forgotten all my "woes." All I wanted to do was help her!

"It's okay, Layla. I don't mean to overwhelm you. I simply want you to know that not only have I lived that life and had those thoughts – I still do. God wants you to know that you are not alone. Not because I've experienced this too, but because He is with you. He understands this emptiness that you feel. Even when things have gone well, and you've had some high moments, you are still longing for *that* dream to be fulfilled."

Heaves of tears spilled from Layla's eyes. Her hands still trembled more than a little bit. Immediately, I grabbed Layla with one hand and snatched my purse from the chair with the other. Hurriedly, I ushered her to the lounge my niece had in the back. It was plush and peaceful. And this was not a moment for spectating eyes. Layla needed a breakthrough and unbeknownst to Layla, so did I.

Watching from another table as she sat other guest, Latrell knew first-hand what was about to happen. She walked to my table and grabbed my lunch. It would be boxed up and ready to go when I was done. She'd also experienced my ministry. There was a day that she too had to be taken to the back away from prying eyes.

In the lobby, Latrell smiled knowing that Layla's life was about to change just as hers did.

CHAPTER FIVE

Bre' was a tall, slender young woman who wore grace like a glove. She boasted long, brown, natural hair that she usually wore straight or pulled back into a neat ponytail. She had one of the biggest and brightest smiles you could ever encounter. It was a family trait that we all shared. Her mom, LaToya and I, had that same smile.

Bre' heard the lounge door open and came out of her office in the back to see who had entered. She knew that it had to be someone who worked for her or me, dropping in to see her. She stopped short at the doorway at what she saw. Immediately, she knew that God was answering the prayers she'd been praying for young Layla since she'd hired her.

When Bre' hired Layla, she knew there was great deliverance and healing that she desperately needed. She also knew, that at some point, I would meet Layla and she prayed that God would speak to me concerning her. It looked like that time had come sooner than she thought it would.

"Thank you, Jesus!" Bre' quietly whispered as she stood in the doorway praying and watching. I was literally laying in the floor with a sobbing and bucking Layla. It was a good thing Bre' had the walls sound proofed. The way she was sobbing and writhing in the floor, someone may have thought that she was being hurt.

Bre' continued to pray in the Spirit, as I prayed, calling out strongholds and demons assigned and attached to Layla's life. She listened and prayed silently as I spoke the word of God over Layla until she began to calm down.

At that moment, Bre' was so glad that she'd dedicated her business to God and told Him to use it as His sanctuary and a place that life, hope and freedom could be found. Yes, in her restaurant! After some rough patches in life, she was determined that her life and everything attached to it would be dedicated and used for and by God.

Bre' briefly walked away from the door. She walked down the hall to the kitchen area to retrieve a few bottles of water. She knew from previous occasions that I would ask for some and wanted to have them nearby. In a way, she felt like she was a ministry partner to me. I was known to flow in my gifts anywhere. For that reason, Bre' was even more grateful that this was a place that it could be done freely and so was I.

Grabbing the bottles of water from the large refrigerator, Bre' asked her staff to steer clear of the lounge for a while today.

"Ms. Maiya is at again, huh?" One of her long-time employees said with a smile.

"Well, you know my saying. Wherever and whenever God wants to work. Whatever He wants to do, we are here for it!"

"Yes ma'am! We are all blessed because of that. I'll make sure no one comes over to that side."

"Thank you," Bre' said exiting the kitchen walking quickly back to the lounge. This time, she walked into the room and closed the door completely for more privacy.

"Perfect timing." I said looking up at her. Reaching for a bottle, I asked, "May I have one of those?"

"Yes ma'am. Do you need anything else?"

"No, just keep praying as you have been. She's going to be fine."

Layla was now laying on the soft, brown leather sofa. Her loud cries had reduced to silent tears and she was finally still. Her breathing seemed to have returned to normal. Her countenance, however, was different.

I turned my focus back to Layla and offered her the bottle of water Bre' had given me. "It will be good for you to drink this to help replenish you."

Layla accepted the water but kept her eyes shielded by her long lashes. She never looked up or made eye contact with Bre' nor me.

I discerned her shame and embarrassment immediately although she did not speak on it. God did not give me the green light to speak on it either. I made a mental note to remember it in prayer. I knew it would take more than just this one day to help Layla fully move into her newfound place of freedom in Christ.

Bre' spoke softly to her. "Layla, you're welcome to take the remainder of the day off. I know you've most likely experienced something very unfamiliar and need time to process it and to rest."

Layla raised her head slightly. "Thank you, Ms. Bre', but I really can't afford to be off right now. I have goals I have to meet so I need to stay on the clock." She sat up quickly, ready to go back to work.

"That's nothing to worry about. You'll be paid for your full shift." She looked toward me saying, "I'll leave you all to finish up. Auntie, lunch is on me today. Love you!"

Layla gasped. "She's your auntie for real! WOW!"

Bre' and I laughed. We got that reaction almost every time.

"Yes, she's really my auntie," she chuckled more. She was tickled by the way Layla's eyes bucked at that realization. "I'll see you bright and early tomorrow morning, young lady," she said turning to leave.

"Yes ma'am. Ms. Bre'?"

Bre' stopped at the door and turned back to us. "Yes?"

"Thank you so much. Thank you for hiring me. You took a chance on me when other people wouldn't. Thank you."

Lord, this baby is about to get our waterworks started.

"You're very welcome. Now, make God and me proud. It's not over for you." With that, she left the lounge and headed back to her office. As she walked, she prayed - *God, thank you for speaking to me about her. I'm so glad I was obedient to your voice. You are a worthy Father.*

CHAPTER SIX

In the lounge, Layla and I exchanged information and talked about what her next steps should be. I reassured her that she would not be alone in her life transition and that she'd have a support system and mentor in me.

"Well, Ms. Layla, are you about ready to go home now?"

"Yes, I think so. I'm still a little fuzzy but I think I'll be okay to make it home. Thank you for praying for me."

"You're welcome. It was truly God who led me to do it. It was my pleasure to serve you."

"May I ask a question?"

"Of course."

"How do you know these things?"

"What do you mean?"

"All the things you were saying when you were praying. They were all true. Some of those things - I've never, ever told anyone." She dropped her head again slightly and barely whispered - "especially about the molestation and rape. How did you know?"

I chuckled a little but quickly turned serious. "It's a spiritual gift from God called Word of Knowledge. I am what the Bible calls a Prophet. God speaks to me and shows me different things that aid me in ministering more effectively to people. In short, God showed me."

"Humph. God said something about me? Wow!"

"Yes ma'am! God knows all about you. Your past, present and future. Just as He speaks to Prophets, He desires to speak to you too."

"Wait, Ms. Maiya," she said hurriedly. "You're taking me way too fast," chuckling. "I think I better go rest. This is a lot! But I promise you, I'm not going backwards. I'm just not ready to hear God talk."

I laughed with her.

"I understand. Trust me, it's a process. As you grow in God and learn about this new life, you'll desire to hear His voice. Until then, we'll focus on strengthening you to be able to walk in your deliverance and healing."

"Yes ma'am. I really want that."

"Alright, let's get you out of here before Ms. Bre' changes her mind," I teased.

"Yes ma'am!"

"I'm going to see Bre', we'll talk soon." I grabbed my purse and exited the lounge through the same door Bre' did.

*****

Layla breathed a long, deep sigh of relief.

Whew, I haven't felt this free in a very long time. I almost don't remember ever feeling this way. I don't know what this is, but I like it. I sure hope it lasts. God spoke about me. Wow! I guess this is real. Wow! Just Wow!

I've never had an encounter with God. I think I'm still reeling from all that I heard Ms. Maiya praying. I would have never thought in a million years that someone would actually know about all of my hidden pains. And I'm still amazed that she said that God loves me and cares about everything that I've been through. And what is this feeling? My mind is so clear. I've never experienced a time, that I can remember, when I didn't have racing thoughts and anxiety.

Wait! The anxiety wasn't there.

Layla stopped in her tracks as she was exiting the building. "Oh my God! Something has really happened to me."

She was talking to herself as she stood there in amazement. "God, you must really be something because I've had anxiety as long as I can remember. I don't even remember a time that I didn't have it. WOW!" She shook her head and finally smiled. "I think I'm going to like this deliverance thing."

Layla made her way to her car, looking forward to going home. That was something she hadn't experienced in a long while either.

Her drive home was uneventful, but she found herself very sleepy. She couldn't wait to get home to her bed. Layla didn't have a full understanding of what happened in that room but what she did know, was that something happened *in* her. She knew she would be different from this day forward.

CHAPTER SEVEN

"Knock, knock!" I stood at the door of Bre's office waiting for the invitation to enter as always. I tried to be respectful of her space even though I'd been told many times that I could just come right in.

Bre' lifted her head, revealing that huge smile again. "Hey, Auntie Prophetess." That was the nickname she always called me. "Please come in and quit standing in that hallway. I've told you a million times - just come on in." We laughed together because this was our usual lighthearted banter when we saw each other.

"You know my rule. I ask to enter and wait for permission. Even in my favorite, brightest, sweetest niece's office." We laughed again because this was my answer every single time. I never changed it.

"Yeah, yeah, yeah," Bre' said through her laughter. "Come on in here. Thank you so much for what you did today for Layla. I knew it would happen one day. I prayed for it! I didn't know it would be so soon."

I raised my right eyebrow at that statement. "Oh, you knew - did you?" I smirked.

Bre' burst out laughing. She almost yelled. "Auntie!!! You never miss an opportunity to pray for somebody! I think you like praying more than preaching and we know you L.O.V.E. preaching and prophesying!

This time, we both laughed loudly. I couldn't deny any of what Bre' said. I was quick to pray and yes, I loved preaching and prophesying the Word of the Lord.

After a few minutes of hysterical laughter, we finally calmed down.

"Seriously, I prayed for her and that she would meet you and encounter your ministry. You know I think you can pray anybody through."

"Well thank you ma'am. Surely God has His own way of doing things and I'm just grateful to be used by Him. It's not always easy and some days are harder than others, but God always comes through. I've just learned over the years to ask Him to do the work and to follow His lead."

"Auntie?"

"Yes?"

"Why do you say the same thing every time?"

Once again, loud laughter erupted from both of us. The look on Bre's face, when she asked that question sounding like a twelve-year-old, was absolutely priceless.

"Because it's always the same, silly girl."

I couldn't help but love this highly intelligent, kindhearted young lady. Her ability to make me laugh in most situations was such a blessing to me.

"I'm about to get out of here. I think I've been on "break" long enough now."

"Well, don't leave your lunch. Latrell had it packed up for you." She walked over to her personal refrigerator in the far-right corner of her office to retrieve it for me. "That girl loves you something fierce. She's going to make it because of how you helped mentor her."

Receiving the decorative bag branded with Bre's Bistro logo on it, I admired the attention that Bre' seemed to put into every detail of her business. I smiled, so proud of how Bre' had grown and evolved into an amazing woman and business owner. I was even more proud that she was Kingdom minded and believed that all things should be done unto the glory of God. *I guess I did impact her after all.*

"Thank you, Sweetness. Please thank Latrell for me. I think I'm going to slip out the back door today."

"Okay, I sure will. She will miss saying goodbye to you, but she will understand. You have literally worked your entire break. Love you, Auntie Prophetess."

"I love you more. I'll see you again soon." I turned to exit the back door attached to Bre's office.

Well alright, Lord, I thought as I rounded the corner of the building onto the sidewalk.

I guess I didn't see that coming because I was so caught up in my woe is me moment. Please forgive me, Lord. Forgive me for being so focused on me and what I feel are issues. I could have missed that, and it would have been all my fault. I'm so sorry, Lord. And thank You for not allowing me to miss that moment with Layla. Thank You for still counting me worthy to be used. Thank You, Jesus!

I really don't want anyone to miss out on encountering You because I'm not in the right place mentally or emotionally. I realize that I must be healed from this place of extreme highs and lows. Father, please stabilize me and help me to walk in the freedom that You gave me years ago. Help me not to return to that low place of self-defeat. It must change today, Lord. Let my story of suffering in silence end today. Help me to share the things that are trying to keep me bound so that I can break free from them. If You give me the opportunity to speak on it, from now on, I will. Get the glory out of where I've been and change me, God. Change me, God. Change me. I'm not a superwoman. I can't do it like this anymore, Lord. Not like this.

CHAPTER EIGHT

My walk back to work was much better than my walk *to* lunch. I arrived back at the office feeling lighter and more determined. The time of prayer and listening to God during my walk back, helped to add more clarity to my mind concerning myself.

*****

As I re-entered the building, my stride was much slower than my exit. My shoulders were not as tight as they previously were. I felt like I could finally make some progress. It's amazing what serving others did for me. I literally came alive in a way that I couldn't explain. I simply loved serving people!

I was met at the door by one of my frantic junior editors.

"Ms. Jackson, I'm glad you're back." He was clearly upset. His face was beet red and his words were spilling out so fast. I had to listen intently to understand.

Placing my hand on his forearm to still his waving arms I said, "Calm down, what's going on?"

"I think we're going to miss the editing deadline for the upcoming magazine release." His eyes were wide with worry.

"Why do you think that?"

"We haven't received all of the articles for this issue and we are one week away. There's no way we can get through all of the necessary edits and send this to the placement group." His words were rushed; his voice was elevated several octaves above his normal speaking tone.

I raised my voice just a tad to get his attention and pull him out of his worried rant. "Jonathan! Calm down!"

Jonathan didn't even hear me; he was so overwhelmed with worry. This was the first time he'd experienced an outsourced writer not meeting their deadline. He was beside himself with concern.

"I just don't understand why someone would miss their deadline. Don't they know this is unacceptable? It throws us all off. We can't work like this. I can't believe we're not going to make the production deadline. I'm so sorry. I should have said something to you sooner." By now, he was frantic and pacing.

Realizing that I was not going to be able to stop him, I let him get it all out. When he finally took a breath, I calmly spoke to him. I was hoping my calm tone would help to calm him.

"Jonathan, calm down. Listen to me. I have the article. I'm doing the edits myself. We will meet the production deadline. I apologize, you weren't told. However, you are correct. Our writers, in-house or freelance, should meet their deadlines. Due to illness, the writer was unable to meet it this time. I approved the late submission and decided to do the edits, so it wouldn't stress you all out. I see that I made a judgment error in not sharing that information with you. Please forgive me and please – breathe!!!"

Jonathan slowly let out a long breath. He hadn't even realized that he was holding it in.

"Whew! Ms. Jackson, I'm so sorry. I'm sure I just threw some form of a tantrum. I'm glad you have it. I really thought we were about to have a problem."

Pressing the elevator button to finally go upstairs, I motioned for

Jonathan to come with me.

"We'll be just fine. This has, however, reminded me of the importance of effective communication and ensuring that information reaches all the team timely. When we get upstairs, please pull the team together in the main conference room. If you were in a panic, I'm sure someone else may be also. I want to reassure everyone that we will make it. I also want to apologize to everyone else. I've been a bit off and it has affected us. I never want that to happen."

"Will do. You are a class act, Ms. Jackson. I'm forever learning from you."

Maiya smiled. "As long as you learn from my good and not so good, then that is a good thing."

"I get it. I get it," Jonathan laughed lightly.

"Alright, give me about 15 minutes and I will meet you all in the conference room."

We parted ways. I went to gather my thoughts for a few moments. Jonathan, to gather the team.

CHAPTER NINE

I was thankful that I made it to my office without being stopped. I quickly closed and locked my door. Leaning against the back of the door, I let out a long breath and did a few neck-stretches. I had picked up Jonathan's anxiety. It added to what I was already carrying.

"Whew, Lord, I really have to get it together. I don't think I can handle another rattled staff member right now. Bless his heart, he was truly shaken. But I am grateful to have people who love this vision as much as I do and understand the importance of it. Lord, please continue to pull me out of this place so that I don't negatively affect them or the vision you've given me."

I took a few more deep breaths and made my way over to my desk. My office was the one place that I usually loved to be in the building. It was extremely spacious and for the most part, peaceful, despite the sometimes-frigid cold air. Since I spent so much time in there, I normally kept candles and sweet-scented air fresheners plugged in. That lent to that peace. The mahogany furniture that was already in the office when I moved into it, perfectly suited my personality and style. I inhaled the calming lavender scent in my office and allowed it to further soothe me. And finally, someone turned on the heat.

I pulled out my calendar and note pad and made a few notes of what I needed to share with the team, including my humble apology. I was in a much better place mentally than when I left the office earlier.

Maybe I'll give them the remainder of the day off once we're done meeting.

I paused to simply thank God. Earlier that day, I couldn't seem to form a clear thought and I was extremely unproductive. Nothing was coming together. As I sat reflecting on my morning and lunch time, I was certain that God was with me even when I was far from Him.

God, I truly don't know why or how you could ever want to use someone like me, but I am absolutely grateful and completely humbled. I know I'm not worthy at all.

"Not worthy at all, God, but I thank you."

Checking the time on my Fitbit band, I knew I needed to hurry. Everyone was probably gathered and wondering what was going on. It was unlike me to not beat them to the room anytime they were called together. After all, I was a stickler for time. I grabbed my notepad and calendar with an added pep in my step. I didn't want to keep them waiting any longer. In that moment, I felt like I could do this! Actually - like I could do anything.

CHAPTER TEN

"Hey, hey team! I apologize for making you all wait," I said immediately as I entered the door.

The room was a buzz with lighthearted banter amongst the staff. Their attention switched to me upon hearing my voice.

"Thank you all for gathering on such short notice. There was an incident earlier that prompted this impromptu meeting."

"Uh-oh, who did it?" asked one of the young men in the room. It was Thaddeus. He was always the comedian in the group. Even now, his question garnered laughter from the group.

"Relax, nobody did it. Well, actually, it was me."

"Huh?" A few people responded simultaneously.

"It seems that I owe you all an apology. Earlier today, Jonathan came to me and he was in a major place of panic. I failed to communicate to you all that I had the last article that we've been waiting on. I have been editing it but none of you knew that. That's my bad." Occasionally, I used slang and my staff loved it. Literally, the whole room burst into laughter.

"Ah, whatever, y'all. Y'all know I gotta lil' hood in me." At that, they were howling in laughter. I couldn't help but join in with them.

"Ms. J, that's hilarious. I can't deal with you and this slang. Who taught you this stuff? Literally, there is no way possible there is even a little bit of a little bit of hood in you," Johnathan said. Although now he spoke in a much calmer tone and slower pace.

"Oh, but for real, she's got it now. She's the bomb.com on all levels but she will pull one on you." My business manager and partner, Angie, chimed in. She'd been with me the longest, so she could definitely attest to that statement.

"Say what now? I can't believe it," someone else laughed.

"Yeah, yeah," I chuckled more. "That girl is in there; I just try to keep her in check. Alright, let's get back to this meeting so you all can get going for the day."

Loud cheers! Very loud cheers - came from everyone.

There was nothing like getting off work early on a Friday and being off on Monday for a holiday. It was clear they forgave me for the lack of communication! Finally, the laughter and cheering stopped. I shared the remaining items on my list and released everyone to enjoy their weekend.

*****

Finally leaving the office for the day, Angie saw that I was still there. She popped her head in my door before she headed to the elevator.

"So, you're going to give everybody else the remainder of the day off and not take it for yourself?" Angie smirked at me like only she could.

"Oh, you're one to talk." I quipped back, looking at the treble clef shaped clock on my wall. "Looks like I'm not the only one."

"Oh, no ma'am! I'm on my way out the door at this very moment," she said waving and walking away. "Go home, Maiya. As you said, we're going to make it," she yelled back over her shoulder.

"Yeah, yeah- I'm going," I yelled back. I smiled. I was grateful that

Angie was still with me after all these years. In business, ministry and life.

I'm going just as soon as I finish these last edits. Lord, help me to stop taking on these extra duties when I don't have to. I really thought it was a good idea and would be helpful but, I am tired! I'm going to make it happen for the team though. Just one more paragraph and I'll be done.

*****

Forty-five minutes later, I finally finished editing the article and sent it to the placement unit. I could shut it down and head out the door. Of course, I felt like I had so much more work to do when I got home but this part was finished for now. After shutting down my computer, I grabbed my purse and prepared to leave. I realized I had a certain pep in my step that wasn't there earlier today.

I was grateful! A smile flooded my face! It was time to go home.

Maybe I'll enjoy some down time as well on these days off.

CHAPTER ELEVEN

As I exited the building, I said good night to the night shift security guard and headed to my car. I could hear my phone ringing with my song, *"I'm Free"* playing, but I just let it ring. I would check it when I got settled in the car. Everybody was gone from work, so it couldn't have been too urgent.

Or so I thought!

*****

Sitting in the car, I had not started the engine yet. I was reflecting on the day and the many emotions that I'd experienced since that morning before I arrived at work.

What a day it had been! Immediately, I felt the urge to pray! I really thought it was about me and the highs and lows I'd been feeling lately. I was off!

"I prayed, Lord, thank You for all of it. It didn't all feel good, but I know that somehow, it's all for my good. I'm not saying that I'm - all better, but I am grateful that You didn't allow me to stay in that same place all day long. Even though You had to use the need of someone else to pull me out, I'm grateful that You did."

And that's where my prayer abruptly shifted! It wasn't about me.

"I pray that Layla is resting in You and that You will guard her from the certain attack of the enemy. I know the devil doesn't like deliverance. His goal is to keep Your people in bondage, but I decree in Jesus name that Your word is true concerning her. Whom the Son sets free, is free indeed. She will not be entangled in that bondage again. She will remain in You. She will remain free. Her soul shall be anchored! Satan, the Lord rebuke you and the blood of Jesus be against you. Layla is secured by the blood of Jesus! Layla is no longer your agent, but she has been bought with the blood of Jesus! Father, I thank You, that You hear me, and You are concerned about Your daughter and You have her covered and protected. I thank You that these words will not fall to the ground, but You are employing the angels that You've given charge over her to keep her in all of her ways. Right now, they are dispatched to her to quench the fiery darts and to keep her from falling, in Jesus name! Glory be to God!"

I began to worship the Lord as I prayed! I felt the heaviness lift and heard my phone ringing again. This time I reached into the outer pocket of my purse and grabbed it.

"Hello," I said, still semi in worship but feeling that it was necessary to answer.

"Ms. Jackson. It's Layla."

"Hi Layla, I was just praying for you!" I think I was almost shouting in excitement about the fact that it was her calling.

Her words rushed out. "Thank God! I almost messed up! I was ready to cuss somebody out and cut them up! I mean I was literally about to cut my baby daddy into a million, cazillion pieces.

He tried me! I told him - no more! I'm not sleeping with him anymore. I'm not fighting with him anymore. But he kept pushing.

He wouldn't go away. He wouldn't leave me alone.

I was on the verge of snapping and then all of a sudden - he just walked away.

Oh my God, I've never seen anything like that before in my life. I always have to fight with him. He is always calling me out of my name and saying that I belong to him. He has never walked away. Oh, no! Do you think that means he's coming back worse? Oh no, I just can't deal with this!"

The more she talked, the louder her voice got. I didn't interrupt her. I let her get it all out. The more she talked, the more I knew that God had just intervened and interrupted the plan of the enemy.

"Ms. Jackson - today was so amazing. I came home, and I slept for so long. I woke up feeling like I'd slept for days! My mind felt so clear! I was cleaning up my house and then this clown comes over here talking all this noise. Ms. Jackson, I'm telling you, I'm quiet and I mind my business and don't bother anybody but there is a side to me that is lethal. I was going to do something to him today. I felt like, I'm not about to let him take from me what I got today. I was ready to fight! Did I mess up? Is God mad with me? Am I still saved? I'm sorry, I know I'm just rambling on and on."

When I heard her take a few breaths, I jumped in to reassure her and try to calm her down.

Speaking slowly and in a calm tone, I told her, "First, calm down. Second, yes ma'am – you're still saved and no, God is not mad at you. Take some more deep breaths, that was a lot."

I cranked my car and continued to talk with her as I started my drive home.

"Let me first say, thank God for what He did for you earlier today. Thank God that He allowed you to rest and your mind to continue to be clear. Now – what you just experienced was two things. One, it was an attack of the enemy or the devil, because that's what he does, especially when you've been through such a deliverance as yours. And second, you just experienced God interrupting the plan of the enemy on your behalf."

"What does that mean?" Layla asked. Her tone had returned to normal, but she was still speaking very fast.

"That means that the devil sent your children's father to disturb your peace and to get you to revert back to your old ways. The fact that the enemy came so quickly to attack your deliverance and salvation is a clear indication that you will pose a threat to the enemy as you continue to learn and grow in your walk with Christ."

"A threat? Me? How? What am I going to do?"

I was too tickled at the anxious way she rattled off those questions, but I explained what I meant.

"Yes, baby girl. A threat. The change that God has already made in you and will continue to make means that you will no longer be an agent for the enemy. You are no longer available to do the enemy's bidding and to operate from an evil, dark place.

You dedicated your life to Christ and declared that you would live for Him. That means that Satan was kicked out. The place that he held in your life and thought he ruled, is no longer available to him.

You are now in position to overcome his attacks, his tricks, and to overcome him. That makes you a threat.

You're also a threat because God is going to use your testimony to help bring others like you to Christ. You're going to be a drawing agent because the changes in you will be so evident that people everywhere will see them. They will want to know what happened to you. That will be your opportunity to share with them what Christ has done and is doing in your life and for you."

"Ohhhh Ms. Jackson, my baby daddy kept saying- what's wrong with you? Why do you look like that? Where have you been? You look lighter. What you been doing? You been with somebody else? He was bombarding me with all those questions. Oh my God, does that mean that he saw a change in me already even though he thought it was because of some other person?"

"Yes! That's exactly what that means. He doesn't understand that it's a spiritual, internal and eternal change that has happened and it's showing up on the outside."

"Wow! That's amazing. I've never seen anything like this before in my life. I don't really understand it all and I know I keep saying that but it's just amazing to me. WOW! Is it always going to be like this?"

I was tickled. She was so excited but so serious.

"Well, if you mean, will people always see what is going on with you? Sometimes, yes? Other times, people may see it but refuse to acknowledge it. But there's something else you should know as well."

"Yes ma'am, I'm listening." She spoke eagerly.

"The enemy will always attack you and tempt you. That's his job. I want to give you a scripture to read and learn because it warns you of the enemy's attack, but it also prepares you for the victory that Jesus has for you."

"Okay, I got my journal just like you said. I'm going to write it down."

"Very good! I'm glad you heeded that instruction. This is an example of why you need it. The scripture is John 10:10 – "The thief comes only to steal, kill and destroy; I have come that they may have life, and have it to the full."

"I'm also giving you an assignment."

"Yes ma'am. I'm nervous."

"No need to be nervous. As you read and learn this scripture, break it down and look up the different words in the verse such as steal, kill and destroy. This will help you to understand exactly what the enemy is trying to do to you. Then look up the word life. This will help you to understand what Jesus has come to give you. Knowing these things will help you to walk in victory and to be reminded that what Jesus came to give you is greater than what the enemy will attempt to do to you.

I call this – word study. It's not just knowing the scripture but it's important to understand it as well. I'm very glad that you called and shared this experience with me. I know that was probably hard for you to do because establishing trust is not always easy."

"It wasn't easy," Layla responded, "but I was overwhelmed. I thought I'd take a risk and call you since you said that I could. I'm so glad we talked. I know you're busy, so I won't take up anymore of your time. I'm going to do my homework. Thank you, Ms. Jackson. Thank you so much!"

"You're very welcome. To God be the glory. This was an even better ending to my workday. I'll talk to you soon. Do that assignment, it's going to help you."

"Yes ma'am. I will."

With that, we hung up the phone and I continued my drive home. I spent the rest of the drive listening to my Spotify prophetic worship playlist and worshipping God for His great power and love for us. Yet again, I was amazed that God would consider using me.

CHAPTER TWELVE

"Good Morning, I'm here to see Dr. Corey. I'm Maiya Jackson. I called earlier about being seen today."

The older gray-haired woman stood to her feet with her left hand outstretched toward me. She smiled wide and beautiful. There was something peaceful about her.

"Yes ma'am. I know who you are. I've been following your powerful ministry for many years."

My face remained neutral, but I was shocked. I was good at that. I learned how to not show my emotions or reactions on my face. I did finally smile at her.

"Thank you so much for your support. It is an honor to have served you."

"Served me! She clapped her hands together quickly. "Ms. Jackson, your ministry helped save my life! You may not remember but you spoke healing to my body. The doctors said that I was going to die but after you prayed for me and introduced me to Jesus - I've been well ever since. I'm a miracle because you allowed God to use you!"

By this time, her hands were lifted, and she was almost in full praise mode! I was alright with it! I let my guard down a little as she shared her testimony. I was thanking God with her for her healing and praying simultaneously for mine.

I wasn't physically ill but emotionally and mentally - I was over it. I had spent the entire weekend crying and trying to talk myself out of this dark, depressed state that I just couldn't seem to fully escape.

I found myself thanking God that no one called and needed anything because I felt like I had nothing to give. I really couldn't understand how my highs were so high and my lows so low.

And they happened so close together.

Yesterday, I decided that it was past time to talk to someone. I asked myself how much longer I was going to suffer in silence when help was available to me.

I had to get over myself and whoever I thought I was. I needed help and I needed release.

Her excited voice pulled me out of my thoughts of what led me there that day.

"Ms. Jackson, I just need you to fill out these new patient forms and then we can get you to the back to see Dr. Corey."

"Yes ma'am. Thank you," I responded as I received the clipboard and forms from her.

As I sat filling out the paperwork, I had to keep my tears from falling and ruining the papers. I had my head lowered more than normal because I just wasn't ready for anyone else to see my tears.

I was also ashamed and embarrassed.

I was literally wondering why God would allow me to walk into a therapist office and run right into someone I'd ministered to. My mind was racing.

I just have to hold it together until I get to the back alone. I can't believe that I can't even go anywhere to get some type of relief or help without seeing or meeting someone that I've ministered to. Really, God? Really? I'm so embarrassed that I'm even here.

I really should just leave. This is just crazy that I'm supposed to be Your preacher and prophet but I'm sitting here unable to even get through a clipboard of papers because I'm jacked up. Lord, help me!

Just as I was having the thought and seriously considering walking out, a nurse opened the door and called for me.

"Ms. Jackson, you can come to the back with me. Once you finish your paperwork, I'll bring it back to the front."

I picked up my black Coach purse and quickly followed her to the back. My head was still lowered; I made minimal contact. Once the door closed, she stopped and introduced herself.

"Ms. Jackson, I'm Erica. I heard Ms. Gloria almost shouting her testimony and it prompted me to come up front. She talks about you often and all of us love your ministry. Once I realized who you were, I immediately came to get you to protect your privacy."

My head snapped up! I looked at her with huge tears in my eyes. I was shocked.

I mouthed the words *thank you* to her. At the moment, it seemed like I couldn't find my voice to speak. I was overwhelmed with gratitude. And quite frankly, I was amazed.

It seemed that the Father had me on His mind yet again. If only I could take continuous comfort in that. Maybe I wouldn't be experiencing this debilitating depression that was trying to take me out. Yes, I was aware of it. No, I wasn't handling it well.

Erica smiled knowingly and led me to the room where I would meet Dr. Corey. As she was leaving the room, she paused as if she wanted to say something. Finally, she closed the door and left me to finish the paperwork.

The room was soothing with natural earth tones and a few oranges and soft blues. Everything about the room said relax but that's exactly what I couldn't do.

The plush cream-colored sofa was full of the softest pillows. Throw blankets were draped across each end. The orange and bluish colored rug looked like I could just lay down in it. The circle pattern reminded me of a book that I'd read several times about drawing the circle. Even the pictures on the wall were comforting.

As I perused the room, I saw scriptures on the wall and on some of the paintings. The one that was directly in front of me, as I sat on the sofa, assured me that I was in the right place. It was John 10:10. The same one that I shared with Layla just a few days earlier.

Suddenly, the door swung open and Dr. Corey walked in jovially. "Good Morning, Ms. Jackson. I'm Dr. Corey. How can I serve you today? I've cleared two hours for you so there's no need to feel rushed."

First of all, let's just say that Dr. Corey; *she* was not what I expected. The last thing I wanted to do was pour out my whole life and soul to a woman. I thought *yeah, I should have left*. I felt myself going back into that shell just that quick.

"Ms. Jackson, before you decide to pack up and leave, give me a shot. It won't be as bad as you think."

I just looked at her. I still hadn't said anything. By this point, I was pleading with God to give me a way out of this. I was thinking that this was just a bad idea.

First, she's a woman. I would have preferred a man. Don't ask me why because honestly, I don't know.

Second, she was this young, beautiful bright eyed, orangish-red haired, full of life woman. And was that some salt and pepper I saw? I thought, she couldn't be that old. I really felt like God was trying to be funny.

Finally, I stood as I spoke. "Dr. Corey, thank you for blocking time for me but I don't think this is a good idea after all. I think I can work through it on my own."

She tilted her head slightly and looked at me and I knew that look! I knew it because I had given it to others before. I was not ready for her response.

"When I was in prayer about this appointment, the Lord told me you were going to try to run. And you can run if you'd like but Prophetess Jackson - you can't hide."

I raised my right eyebrow at that statement. I rarely introduce or refer to myself with titles although many people knew me by them. Whoever this praying woman was, she'd clearly done her research. She continued unphased by my raised eyebrow or flint like face.

"You've done enough of taking care of others and working through it on your own. It hasn't worked.

It's time for your smiling face to stop lying.

It's time to stop being what everybody else needs but not what you need.

You're the prophet not God!

And furthermore, I'm surprised that a prophet such as yourself would walk out on a God set up. I know the woman who drives everybody else's destiny is not about to walk out on her own."

She paused and just looked at me kind of matter of fact like.

"For the record, let me re-introduce myself to you. I'm Prophetess Dr. Corey and God sent you here. So, you can sit down, and we can talk, or you can walk away and have to come back again."

I felt the need to brace myself so I wouldn't fall. It felt like the room started shifting when she spoke this time. That authority came through in a recognizable way. She spoke with heaven's authority. I knew that sound! I knew when God was speaking through someone. I realized that I had just met my match.

Still, I stood there with my eyes locked on her. I had a decision to make in that moment that would affect my life and I knew it. I could walk out and continue the endless cycle of sleepless nights, praying for relief, racing thoughts and feeling empty or I could sit with God's prophet and see what God wanted to do.

She was still standing in her position at the door. She didn't move; she didn't say anything. She just waited for me to decide.

Finally, I dropped my head and plopped back down to the couch. I let my purse slip to my feet. It felt like a ton of weights were on my shoulder and around my legs. It seemed like I'd been standing there staring at her for at least 15 minutes. It probably wasn't that long, but it sure felt that way.

She glided across the room, kicked off her shoes, took her seat across from me in the huge chair and crossed her legs Indian style. And started praying!

"Now that that's settled, welcome to Grace Life Therapy. Your session begins now. Let's talk!"

CHAPTER THIRTEEN

"Whew! That lady is something else! I thought I was a firecracker. Lord, I have met my match today." I slung the car door open and tossed my purse over to the passenger seat as I slid into the driver seat. I sat in the parking lot for about 45 minutes before I pulled out. My mind replayed the last 2 hours I spent talking with Dr. Corey. It was one of the best time investments I'd made in a long time.

"I don't think I've ever told anybody that much about me in such a short period of time. And I really never thought it would feel so good."

I left my phone on silent as I drove home. I didn't even take it out of my purse. I needed to continue processing this journey that I had begun, and I didn't need outside voices at that time.

As I replayed the conversation, I realized that I needed to practice this more often. Meaning, leaving the phone on silent and not answering during times when I needed quiet time for myself.

Talking with Dr. Corey helped me to understand that I needed a healthy relationship with myself. I could not continue to help and sow into others but not give that same level of dedication and care to myself. I saw how I'd put too much emphasis on others and not enough on me.

I was out of control.

All I ever thought about was other people. I had become selfless to the detriment of myself. Instead of correcting it long ago when I realized it, I learned to cope and tried to master it. I labeled it as "what I do." I rationalized that it came with the territory and it was what Jesus would want me to do.

As I listened to myself talk in that office, I literally stopped and said, *"Wait, that's not right. I don't even teach others to do that. I stress the necessity to rest and to recuperate and be refreshed."*

"Uhm! I repent Lord! I've been teaching and preaching something that I have not been doing. The fact is that I've been going so much, taking care of everybody else and worrying about how everybody else was doing that I became a hypocrite." At that moment, I pulled over on the highway right at 20 East and Sigman Road.

I just stopped.

I was literally overcome with guilt. I didn't ever want to be a hypocrite.

I started praying and asking God to please not let me preach Jesus to many but then find myself as a cast away. And then I realized I had another issue.

Fear!

I was praying from a place of guilt and fear.

"I don't want to be a cast away. I don't want to disappoint you. I don't want to be a hypocrite." My words were rushing out and I was probably yelling as if God couldn't hear me.

I slammed my hands against the steering wheel, sobbing.

My hands clenched the steering wheel as I dropped my head.

"GOD!!!" I cried out loud, anguish spilling from my veins.

"How did I get here? Why am I depressed and sitting on the side of a highway alone? How is it that I can help everybody else, but not myself?"

"GOD!!!!"

I covered my face with both hands and leaned back on the seat. I was trying to catch my breath. I was in a full anxiety attack and seemingly unable to collect myself.

I felt alone.

I just sat there.

Tears were streaming down my face; my heart was racing as it normally does when I have an anxiety or panic attack. Immediately, I felt the urge to retreat.

I slammed my car into drive, barely checked my side mirror and shot back onto the highway. I just needed to get home and go to bed. In my mind, when I woke up and started tomorrow, I would be fine.

As I started the remainder of my drive home, I heard my phone repeatedly buzzing in my purse. I ignored it.

The buzzing continued. I continued to ignore it.

I wasn't talking to anybody in the state that I was in. I would not give anybody the opportunity to see me in this place of panic. I had enough of that earlier with the smart mouth, *Prophetess* Dr. Corey. Naw, I'm good!

And I'm not going back! This was supposed to help me, not send me into this place. I should have known better because the process is never pretty, but in this state, my thoughts were not rational.

I heard my phone buzzing again. When I pulled into my garage, I grabbed it to see who was continually calling or texting me like that. When I saw who it was, I slapped my right hand to my forehead, shook my head and just closed my eyes.

I sat in my car another 30 minutes. Just sitting. It was the good doctor.

I didn't answer. Whatever she wanted; she could just leave a message. Or better yet - not.

I finally pulled myself out of the car. I grabbed my purse and searched for the house keys. I was done with this day and these emotions. I was done talking and sharing.

When I unlocked the door, I headed straight to my shower and then to my bed.

I wasn't talking.

I wasn't studying.

I wasn't reading.

There was nothing happening that night! No social media post. No encouraging anybody tonight. Not even myself. I was over it!

When I originally decided to go to therapy, I thought it was a good idea. But this wasn't what I expected.

"Well, I'm not going to think about it anymore tonight. I'm going to bed."

CHAPTER FOURTEEN

Three a.m.

"Really, God! I KNOW You do **not** want me to pray and intercede for anything and anybody. I know You know that I am really messed up. Today was horrible and I just don't have it in me. I'm not the intercessor for anybody tonight." I laid back down in the bed and defiantly snatched the covers over my head.

Two hours later I was still tossing and turning, had not been back to sleep and still hadn't prayed. I sat up in the bed, frustrated by this point because I didn't sleep well when I was asleep. Now, I couldn't sleep at all.

And so... I sat.

In the stillness of the morning, I sat and listened.

It turns out that it wasn't that God wanted me to pray during the watch. He wanted me to listen to Him. I was in such an uproar all day and night that I was missing and almost forfeiting the ministry of the Holy Spirit – to me!

I continued to sit.

I propped my pillows up against my headboard, laid back and listened. I sat there until eight that morning.

God talked to me. I talked to Him. But mostly, He talked to me.

I never picked up my journal that I keep next to the bed as I usually would. But I remembered what God said. The most important thing that remained with me throughout the day was that I needed to change my perspective and let go of my preconceived notions. I was harming myself when God intended good for me. I was inflicting condemnation and self-imposed guilt on myself when God was attempting to move me forward by showing me what was wrong *and* how to correct it.

The unction to go to Grace Life Therapy wasn't coincidental. It was God. He wanted me to know that just as I'd been a safe place for people to recover, heal and release, He had created one for me. He wanted me to see that just as He had commissioned and assigned me to serve people and put me in the right positions at the right time for them, He'd done the same thing for me.

I learned from the Holy Spirit that God won't make you something to someone else that He does not make available to you as well.

What do I mean? I'm sure you probably said - what? It's simple.

As the Destiny Driver and a Spiritual Mother to many, I am a safe place for others to land and heal. People can trust my integrity and character and know that what they share with me will be confidential, covered in prayer and assistance will be provided as needed.

Well, the Holy Spirit had to help me understand and accept that Grace Life Therapy was that place for me. That was not my perception. As a result, I decided I was **not** going back. Chile, I was in my feelings.

I felt like she uncovered all this stuff and made it resurface. And that was the issue! It was resurfacing, which meant it was never gone. It was just suppressed.

Suppressed emotions or masked hurt or pain is not healing. It's a coping mechanism.

Coping mechanisms are not the will of God for our lives. He wants us to be free indeed! God wanted me to experience complete freedom in every area of my life. Not just when I was ministering to others, preaching the gospel or singing.

He would not allow me to be a public success and a private failure. Not in any area. That is love!

After receiving the ministry of the Holy Spirit, I made an intelligent and less emotional decision. My therapeutic journey to freedom from hidden depression and suffering in silence would continue.

I really didn't want to disappoint God. I didn't want to disappoint or misguide the ones He gave me to lead, cover and equip.

This journey was necessary for me because it was necessary for them. In those five hours of the morning with God, I became a priority to me as I realized I was a priority to God.

My ministry was not just a gift to others; it was a gift to me. Because of that, I wanted to give God the best me that I could give Him.

I spent that Saturday quietly in the presence of God, continuing to listen to Him and writing in my journal. Ironically, the front of the journal had the words *I'm Free* written on it.

I finally listened to the voicemail from Dr. Corey. Although she stated that I could call her back that weekend, I decided that I would call on Monday. I accepted that I needed her help, but I knew God was not done talking to me.

For those who are reading this part of my story, consider your perspective of counseling and therapy. Your mindset concerning it may be wrong. It may be a setup from God. And by all means - listen to God. Most times, it's not what we need to say to Him, instead it's what we need to hear from Him that will help us the most.

CHAPTER FIFTEEN

"Good morning, Ms. Jackson, how are you today?" I was anxiously greeted by my favorite, always excited, junior editor - Johnathan.

"Good morning, Johnathan. I'm better. How are you?" I smiled knowing that he was about to unleash a mad, Monday rant on me. Thank God Angie called me to give me a heads up. I was semi-prepared.

"Well, since you asked. I'm not good." His words rushed out as usual. "I just don't understand these writers who can't seem to meet deadlines. I mean seriously, they would be having an all-out hissy fit if we didn't pay them on time. Why don't we just get rid of them or replace them? Oh, we have contracts," he said answering his own question. "But what are the consequences?"

He quickly kept going. "I mean, they are stressing me out. They just don't know that we have so much to do after it reaches us. Can we have a meeting with them or something? I think we need to have one of your come to Jesus meetings, Ms. J. These people just don't seem to get it!" His arms were flailing by this time. His face was flushed!

He finally took a breath, but I didn't say a word. I thought I was going to holler out loud in laughter. The look on his flushed face and those rushed words and flailing arms were hilarious to me.

But he did have a point. Maybe we did need a come to Jesus meeting, but first I needed him to calm down. It was entirely too early for him to be this wired up on a Monday morning. I was still recovering from myself *literally* and I was not ready.

Maybe I should have stayed home today, I thought.

"Ms. Jackson, what are we going to do?" His question snatched me out of that thought.

"*We* aren't going to do anything. But I will. You have several valid points. I will make sure that the writers know they will either meet the deadlines or their contracts will be voided. I am grateful that you have such a great passion and concern for my business and the product that we produce. I don't want you to be stressed or overwhelmed, so I want you to know that I hear you loud and clear and I will take care of it."

"Today!" I reassured him.

The color was finally starting to come back into his face. His breathing was slowing down. I got through to him and reassured him enough so that I could at least make it to my office to deal with this problem once and for all.

Normally, this would have been nipped in the bud long ago. But, in the midst of my sadness, depression and simply trying to make it through the days, I allowed it to go on too long. Enough was enough! I would not have those who labor so fervently with me stressed out because of someone else's laziness or lack of ethics to honor their contract.

I think I had come to an 'enough is enough' place concerning many things. A change was coming and quickly. I wasn't going to die in this! Neither was my company or my ministry.

"Thank you, Ms. Jackson! I know when you have that talk, things will get back in order. Thank you for hearing me out. Even if it was first thing in the morning, before you made it to your office and had your coffee. Thank you!"

"No worries, Johnathan. I'm glad you shared this with me and helped pull me back into the space necessary to address it immediately. I'll make the necessary phone calls and copy you on the emails."

That big, wide grin on his face said it all.

"Alright, go take a break and then let's get back to work and make it happen!" I turned and headed toward the elevator.

"Yes ma'am!" Johnathan walked in the opposite direction headed to the staff breakroom. I usually kept them well stocked with all kinds of snacks and quick meals for the staff.

CHAPTER SIXTEEN

I started those phone calls with the one I thought would be the easiest. This writer was only submitting a one or two -page contribution. Although she primarily submitted her articles on time, the last few had been late. And sometimes, they didn't line up with the vision shared with her when she came on as a writer.

"Hi, Melanie. This is Maiya Jackson from Living With More Publications. How are you today?"

"I'm good. I'm working on that article. I know I promised it would be on time, but I'll be done soon." Her response was rushed.

"That's good. That's what I'm calling to speak with you about. Your submissions."

"What? She snapped. "I just said, I'll have it in soon. You act like you pay me a whole lot for what you get."

I literally looked around my office like - *did this baby just say that to me?* Lord, here we go.

"Melanie, your pay is what you agreed to when you were contracted. So, that's not up for discussion. What is up for discussion is the terms of the contract you agreed to. In the contract, your submission dates for each issue and the type of articles needed were clearly written out. We also discussed them at length to make sure you understood the need to meet the deadlines."

"Look!" She loudly interrupted me. "I don't see what the big deal is." She was enraged. "You got the articles and your magazine came out on time. You made way more after you released it than what you paid me for the article, so this is stupid. I'm not about to be going through this with some *little* magazine."

I could feel the switch happening in me and I didn't want it to.

I wanted this call to be strictly business. I didn't want to discern anyone else's pain or situation. I just wanted to deal with the problem and let that be it. But I couldn't.

It was too heavy, and I had already heard God speak. I let her finish her rant before I said anything further.

"Like seriously, you called me because I am a few days late. Big freaking deal! I'm so sick of this mess. People always want something for nothing or a little of nothing. And have the nerve to act like your magazine is award winning or something."

She was going IN - and OFF! I could literally feel the tension and hear her anxiety. I was about to jump in and stop her, but she started up again just as quick as she took half of a breath.

"And who do you think you are - the gospel Oprah? Lady bye! If you don't want my articles *when* I send them, then I don't have to send them at all. Calling me like you're actually doing something with that lil' fake magazine. And it's only online. People can't even buy a hard copy. Girl, you need to get all the way over yourself and whatever you think you're doing because it is not that serious. Lil' junk probably won't even last. Chile bye."

Y'all know my eyebrows were raised by this time but I couldn't even unleash on her. When the line finally became silent again, I asked her a question that had nothing to do with anything that she'd just said.

"Melanie, how can I pray for you?

Silence.

How can I help you?

More Silence.

I called to talk about your submissions, but that's not really what you need. What do you need?"

Complete and utter – silence!

We had to have held the phone for at least three minutes. I wasn't going to have an all-out brawl with her. I knew that this lashing out was not because of me. I knew because I'd been there before. I wasn't going to let what I'd learned be wasted. Especially, not in a moment like this. I'd learned. I'd grown. I could help... if she let me.

"Melanie," I paused because I heard her. Not speaking but crying. The longer I waited, the louder and the more gut wrenching her cry became. I began to pray as I listened to her pain through her sobbing. There were no words, only loud cries and deep groans.

I began to pray out loud. I didn't pray over her because I didn't want her to think that her pain was not important. I chose those moments when there was a brief silence to pray as she cried.

She cried. I prayed.

She cried. I prayed.

She cried. I prayed.

I don't remember all that I prayed. I only remember asking the Holy Spirit to step in and intercede for His daughter, because I had nothing, but I knew that she needed something. Thirty-five minutes later, she'd stopped crying. I'd stopped praying.

We agreed that we would speak again soon. What God wanted to do was more pressing. I *would* keep my word to Johnathan but first, I had to be obedient to God. Her well-being was more important.

After the call ended, I sent an email to confirm that I would be in touch to schedule our next call. In the email, I listed my concerns and the various methods of resolution that were acceptable for the current problems. I also reiterated the upcoming deadline dates that needed to be met in order for full payment to be received. As promised, I copied Johnathan.

I had other calls to make, however, I took a few moments to myself before I moved on to the next calls. My first thought was, "how do you keep using me, when I am in this place?" That was my question to God.

I decided to take a quick break from my desk, go out onto the floor with the staff and check in with some of them. Sometimes people just need to know that you are there, you are concerned and what they are experiencing is as real to you as it is to them.

I walked the floor for about thirty minutes. I chatted with different people, caught up on their lives and set up some time to speak with them further. Finally, I had to get back to my office and make the last two calls before I called it a day.

CHAPTER SEVENTEEN

I sighed deeply. "Now that those calls are done, I can send this final email." Somewhere during the day, I made a decision for me.

******

July 12, 2019

From: Chamaiya Jackson

To: All Staff

Re: Leave

Greetings All,

It's been an eventful first half of the year for us. We've had some amazing highs and some challenging lows. Through it all, you've been more than loyal to this God given vision. For that, I am so grateful. As we prepare to release our next issue, I am so grateful for your hard work, dedication and the occasional frantic raves of panic. It's been a journey, but a good one! This next issue is going to be one for the books!

Many of you don't know that I've been experiencing extreme depression. I know that I've been functioning, however, that's simply not enough. I will not be the person that pushes you to greatness, empowers you to be all that you're supposed to and serve in excellence and not do it myself. That would be a disservice to you, me and this company that you've given so much time and talent to.

Your labor of love is more appreciated than any of you know. When I first envisioned having a magazine and a company, you all came on board fully believing in what this could be and the impact it could make. You trusted me with your livelihood. I don't take it for granted. Because of you, this company is flourishing and this year we've seen some of our highest numbers so far!

I say so far because I truly believe that there is more to come! God has something so amazing for this company and each of you who have committed to working the vision.

With that said, I'm expecting that you will continue in the same manner as you have. Let's continue to produce a great product and serve the people who need us most!

Effective immediately, I will be on leave until further notice. You will have limited access to me via phone and email. During this time, Angie will be leading you. She has been with us since the inception and is well versed in every aspect of this company. Please go to her first before reaching out to me. She will be able to provide you with any assistance that you may need! She has full authority to handle and make decisions on all things regarding the company. I'm confident that each of you will flourish under her guidance. I believe in her - and you!

I am taking this time for therapeutic reasons. I'll be meeting with my new therapist and working through the vast list of things that have caused me distress and pushed me further into a depressed state. It's time for me to take care of me. As much as I love caring for others, I must dedicate some real time to myself and my overall health.

Please know that you have been a continual source of joy for me, your jobs are secure, and I'm looking forward to returning to you better than I've ever been before. And don't forget that 2020 is the year that we go LIVE with our print editions! Let's get ready to bloom!

With Love

CHAPTER EIGHTEEN

Monday, July 15, 2019

"Well good morning, Ms. Jackson. It's good to see you again." The twinkle in Ms. Gloria's eyes said that perhaps she was surprised to see me again.

But then again, who knows. The gray- haired receptionist was just as pleasant during my first visit. Actually, she was ecstatic during that visit when I learned that I had once ministered to her.

"Good morning, beautiful! It's good to see you as well. I have an appointment with Dr. Corey today."

"Yes ma'am, she is ready to meet with you. I'll let her know that you are here."

As she got up to go notify Dr. Corey that I was there, I realized that I was the only person in the waiting room that morning. I was glad. I didn't feel like I needed to hide so I wouldn't be seen or recognized. I knew I needed to be here, but I wasn't quite ready for more people to recognize me. I'd tell this story publicly when I was ready, and I simply was not ready yet. I needed time to process my emotions and thoughts and figure out what direction I was going.

I needed the time to come to grips with the fact that I needed this to save my life before it was shared with the world.

Nurse Erica interrupted my thoughts to let me know that Dr. Corey was ready to see me. I couldn't help but notice that she seemed to be glowing today and her makeup was fabulous!

I'll have to remember to ask her about her makeup. Those colors are gorgeous, and the application is flawless.

*****

As I entered the room to meet with Dr. Corey, the walls seemed to close in on me. It was the same, calm scenery as before, but my thoughts were running a thousand miles a minute and all of a sudden - I was hot. Then I was cold. Beads of sweat popped up on my neck. The room felt like it was spinning. I wasn't ready. I thought I was.

I kept running my hands through my hair and twirling my purse. I was literally trembling.

Lord, I am a mess!

I felt like I was about to lose it!

Maiya! Breathe! You can do this! You have to do this for you! No more delaying it. No more running. Breathe.

I stood locked in the spot just behind the closed door of the room for what seemed like an eternity. I took long, slow, deep breaths to bring myself back into focus. I would not allow the enemy to use panic attacks and anxiety to push me backwards.

I was here. I would not retreat. I knew too much about pushing beyond the brink, pressing beyond the obstacles, and all of that jazz.

Somehow, *this* seemed different. It *was* different.

I finally sat down on the long, plush ivory colored couch. All I could do was cover my face, lean my head back for a few seconds and breathe. I was determined, I was going to do this! For me!

CHAPTER NINETEEN

When she walked in the room, I stilled myself. I set my face like flint. Immediately - I was convicted. She chuckled and I knew that she knew. Her words confirmed it.

"Well hello again Prophetess Maiya." Her eyes twinkled. "For the record, we are all glad you've *fully* embraced the full call on your life." I looked at her when she said that knowing exactly what she was referring to. She didn't bat an eyelash. This time - it was *her* face that was set like flint. I knew not to even challenge it.

"It's good to see you even if you were ready to play the tough cookie again today. What changed your mind? Or should I say – your Holy Ghost works!" She laughed.

Even I had to laugh at that. I could tell she'd been checking me out. You have to know me to know that I always say, my Holy Ghost works on me too. That means I'm just as convicted, and I hear God concerning myself too.

"Hello Prophetess Dr. Corey," I said amidst my laughter.

God!!! It felt so good to genuinely laugh!

It felt so good... until I caught myself. Sadly, I got caught up in my thoughts just that quick!

Wow! How sad is that? When was the last time I genuinely laughed, in the moment, outside of work? This thing is worse than I thought. I really need some help.

She cleared her throat, interrupting my thoughts. "Let's start right *there.*"

"Right where?" I feigned.

Yes, I sure did. I acted like I didn't know exactly what she meant. I don't know why I was making the process so hard.

She raised her right eyebrow at me as she crossed the room and took her seat.

"Well, let's not. Let's go this route. I listened to this message that really helped me a few days ago and I want to share a snippet of it with you. It was really enlightening and as you know we are a faith based therapeutic center."

Okay, now she was speaking my language. I was always ready for the revelation of God through His Word. But… I wasn't ready!

She grabbed the small, black remote on the nearby oval, cherry wood end table. She clicked play and that's when I heard it.

"Do you really surrender all?

We must understand that the word all means: the whole of; ones' whole interest, energy. It means fully, entirely, totally, everything. And that word surrender means – to yield to the possession or power of another. To give oneself up to some influence, course, emotion. To submit.

As we look at the posture of Jesus as He speaks His last word before He breathes His last breath on Calvary's Hill, He has taken the position of surrender."

She clicked a button and another snippet played.

"Jesus said to His Father – into Your hands I commit my Spirit. In other words, I'm giving you back what's yours anyway. I commit my spirit. I'm putting myself, my life, my death, my obedience - in your hands. I surrender all. Not just those things that separate me from you, but everything.

Surrender is about knowing and acknowledging that every part of me belongs to God. Most times when someone refers to surrendering to God, they are calling them out of a place of sin. However, surrender goes far beyond sin. Or they are saying give your life to God, live for Jesus. But I submit to you today that many people have accepted Jesus as their Lord, they have confessed it with their mouth that He is Lord. They believe in their hearts that God raised Him from the dead, yet, they still have not surrendered. I told you earlier that surrender means the whole of, ones' whole interest, energy. It means fully, entirely, totally, everything. So, we're saved, sanctified, Holy Ghost filled, fire baptized, but we still want to be in control. To surrender ALL means, we have to give up control of any and everything in our lives. Good and bad. It means that God is in control of the whole of our lives. We don't make decisions without Him. He is not just a guiding factor; He is the guide. To surrender ALL means God, I trust you to do what you said you were going to do."

I sat quietly listening but not making eye contact with her. She clicked play once again.

"Often, we only want to release to God what we can't handle but God wants it all! Surrender is not just for hard times or hard things; surrender is for all things. Jesus said, I commit my Spirit. That means - God, everything about me, internally, externally and eternally, I turn it over to you. I'm no longer trying to guide my life. I'm no longer holding onto the things that I think I'm good with, that I think I can handle. That I think I have control of. But God I give it ALL to you! So, here's the self-check moment of this Good Friday, when was the last time you trusted God with YOU? When was the last time you said, Father, into Your hands, I commit my spirit?"

"Okay, Okay!" My hands were literally lifted, palms facing her in *surrender*. I could not believe that this lady was playing my message back to me. Well actually - I could. That was just like something I would do!

"I see you've really been checking me out," I said. "You've made your point and you're absolutely right."

"I didn't say it. You did." Her face was still set like flint. She meant business. "For the record, I have all day. I had them clear the entire day to make sure that you were comfortable when you walked through those doors. I didn't want you to feel ashamed or worried about people recognizing you. And also, for the record, I've followed your ministry for a while, and I heard this message when you delivered it. It was just as powerful then as it is now. When God brought it back to my remembrance, I knew He would lead me in how and when to use it." She relaxed her face and crossed her arms.

"Are you ready?"

I was speechless. I felt some type of way. Yet I was humbled and honored at the same time. Clearly this woman was tapped into the Holy Spirit. And clearly God sent me here. And clearly, I needed to get over myself. Quickly!

"I was shocked at how long it had been that I genuinely laughed." My statement was the answer to her original place that she suggested that we start the session.

"Now, we're headed somewhere," she said. "That's where you went when I walked in. Your laughter stopped so quickly. It was almost like you either didn't recognize it or you were caught off guard by it."

"Probably a little bit of both," I admitted.

"How did you get here? And by here, I don't mean - not laughing. But here as in this whole place that you're in. I know some of your story. I read your first and second book. But what I don't know is how did you get here after all that you *have* overcome? We need to start there and work our way forward."

I just shook my head and surrendered all. This lady had done her homework and fortunately and unfortunately for me, there was absolutely no getting around it. I was going to have to lay it all on the table.

I sighed so deeply because I knew there was no other way but this way. Tears welled up in my eyes and once again, I refused to let them fall. I clasped my hands together, squared my shoulders and just let it go.

"I bounced back," I answered. "At least for a while. I threw myself into building strong leaders, raising up prophetic people and pouring my all into them. Then, I got back into the routine of traveling, preaching, praying, prophesying and started some businesses. I pulled myself together. I had to. What else was I going to do? I'm Chamaiya Jackson, Daughter of Thunder. The Destiny Driver. So, if I'm honest - As the song by Shekinah Glory says, *'I'm in ministry but I'm messed up. I'm confused with no one to talk to. I need a breakthrough.'*

What I was able to release into the lives of others seems to have escaped me. Most days I feel like, I've given up and nobody even knows. All people see is the gift. And I'm grateful for it, but I need the One who gave me the gift to do something for me. I've been superwoman. Hell, I've been every woman. I'm the go to. The come to. The intercessor. The prophetic voice."

Dr. Corey sat quietly listening and taking notes. She was also audio recording. I consented to that during my first visit when I completed the new patient forms.

"Did you know I started three churches?" I didn't wait for an answer.

"I started three churches in three states. One person didn't accept the assignment until 3 years later. One person kept starting and stopping their Bible study sessions. And nobody showed up for my services. Well, not nobody, but very few. I preached to an empty building once. And I mean preached like it was full. I still ask myself was that faith or foolishness. Most other weeks, I preached to one person. The sad part is, people claimed to be a part of the church and never showed up. Not once. People joined and decided it was just too far to drive. And as soon as I left the building, somebody came at me with 'hey, what time is service? I was thinking about coming out there this week. Girl, bye! No, you were not! I was in a building two years and all of a sudden, *now* you want to come."

I covered my face, ran my hands through my hair and blew out a short breath. But I kept talking. I refused to stop. I was afraid that if I didn't keep talking, I'd lose the nerve.

"And I started two businesses. I don't even know what I even thought I was doing. Who am I to run businesses? For years, very few people bought my magazines. I was so embarrassed. I spent hours and hours working on this magazine. I was so proud of it and when it was ready for sale - nothing. Not even the people who claimed to support me and said- *oh, you should have a magazine. You know your newsletter is just about a magazine anyway.* Humph! Pretty much like the church folks. *When you gonna start your church? We need you. I'm going to be right over there with you.*"

I felt anger but I didn't even try to hide it.

"I'm so over people." My tone shifted. I was more than angry. I heard something in me that I'd easily recognized in others and by the raised right eyebrow on Dr. Corey's face, so did she. But I didn't stop!

"And do you know how many people I've supported? Conference after conference after conference. Showing up. Sowing seeds. Sharing flyers. Pushing others' events. And because I didn't call them to be on my conference agenda, my platform - they did not show up. I'm talking about NONE OF THEM! And they had the nerve to talk down about it.

I wish I could count the number of times I heard, *"I wish I could come." "Uhm, that cost too much." "Oh, I'm going to make it next year." "Oh, I'm praying for you, Sis."* Don't Sis Me!!! Miss me with all that! I'm sick of it!!

I don't owe anybody anything. I don't ask anybody for anything. And I SHO ain't asked for nobody's platform. If you know me, you know this - If God doesn't call your name, I'm not calling it and you ought not call me if He didn't call mine. I'm not swapping platforms and pulpits.

That's some immature, childish *ish* that Chamaiya Jackson does NOT do! And don't get me started on these so-called "sisterhoods" and "networks." Chile bye! A bunch of cliques is more like it. It's all a bunch of mess. And before you ask me if I'm jealous - nah boo! I'm just sick of mess all in the name of the Lord. I'm sick of people doing whatever they want to Maiya and thinking it's supposed to be okay. I'm supposed to keep going. I'm supposed to just overlook it. I'm supposed to be okay with you always asking somebody to sow into your stuff, share your stuff, subscribe to your stuff, yada yada yada!!!!"

By this time, I was in a full yell and full of anxiety! I was really yelling…and trembling. I paused, looking around confused and thinking - *what the world?* I couldn't believe it.

At some point, I had stood up. I didn't even remember getting up. I felt like I was outside of myself. My hands were shaking like leaves. The anxiety was clearly visible. And so was my anger.

I immediately stood still. I blew out a long breath. I dropped back to the couch with slumped shoulders. My next words sounded just like I felt.

"But you feel like mine isn't good enough. Maiya is far from jealous. Maiya is tired."

I felt defeated.

I had started speaking of myself in third person. My voice had lost its' fervor and strength. I was exhausted. Just thinking about how I felt exhausted me. Talking about it seemed to be breaking me even more.

I dropped my head. My long, natural hair fell to the sides of my face, semi shielding my eyes. I closed my eyes and tears immediately dropped to the floor. I tried catching my breath that still seemed shallow. I didn't feel like I could keep talking but more words flowed out. More choppy, staccato like, almost incoherent words.

"More than tired, I'm broken. I'm bitter. I'm more than angry. I'm so disappointed. I'm discouraged. I'm hurt. I feel alone. I'm…I'm depressed." There - I said it.

And then I was silent. In my silence, I immediately recognized that I was also battling unforgiveness. I had not yet truly forgiven in my heart.

Tears fell from my eyes like a rushing waterfall. They were uncontrollable. They were finally escaping that locked up vault they'd been in for years. Years of sucking it up. Years of keeping it moving. Years of making it happen. Years of pressing through it. Years of everyone else being a priority. Years of being everybody's cheerleader. Years of pushing and serving everybody.

Years. And years. And years.

I don't know how long I sat with my head down. It felt as heavy as bricks. Dr. Corey never said a word. When I finally lifted my head, I clasped my perfectly manicured hands together and shrugged my shoulders.

"That's how."

CHAPTER TWENTY

"Jesus! That was a lot. I'm exhausted. I didn't think I was still holding that. I had made up my mind to move forward, support or no support. When did it resurface?"

Those were my thoughts as I sat in my car after the very intense session at Grace Life Therapy. Dr. Corey was extremely patient but very firm. I talked through things today that I truly thought were behind me. One day, I'll be able to share those things from a healed place.

"I think I'm better leaving this session than I was the last time. That's important to me. I want to get better."

After sitting for a few more moments, I decided to treat myself to a late lunch. Originally, I headed to Bre's, my favorite place, but I decided against it. I needed to go to a place that I wasn't known and there would be no expectation of me.

"That reminds me, I need to reach out to my mentees and sons and daughters in ministry and officially notify them of my Sabbatical."

As soon as I made it to JemiCole, a new restaurant I'd been wanting to try, I parked and sent a message via email to them.

*****

From: Maiya Jackson

To: The Covenant Crew

Re: Sabbatical

Greetings My Loves,

I pray that all of you are well! I'm so proud of the great work you are doing in the Kingdom! We've had a tough but great first half of the year. We have so much work to do however it's time for me to pause, take a breather and regroup.

Today, I had my second visit to Grace Life Therapy. Yes, I've made the decision for therapy. While I'm a strong advocate for prayer and I've always encouraged you to speak to a licensed therapist, I had not taken the step. Well, I'm taking my own advice. Along with therapy, I'm also taking a sabbatical.

This will allow me time to work through my healing process. This will ensure that we can all move forward in the power and purpose that God intends for us. I will be available; however, it will be limited.

I solicit your prayers as I endeavor to walk out this journey God has for me.

Leaders of Destiny Worship Center International: Keep leading well as usual. A ministry rotation schedule for the Staff Pastors and Ministers will be sent later this week. This will be helpful to you all as our staff ministers will have the opportunity to minister during this time. I will be teaching the group training sessions that I've already scheduled for this month. I am confident that you are all trained and equipped to handle our weekly services and bible studies as well as the organizational functions of the church.

Covenant Fellowship Pastors and Leaders: I will not be conducting one on one sessions for the next two months. You are free to email me, and I will respond. I will be available via phone for limited conversations. As I stated above, all the group training sessions scheduled will be conducted this month. I encourage you to intentionally make plans to meet us onsite or in our private group.

Mentees: I will see you this week and next week for our scheduled sessions.

Once I've finished these sessions and meetings, I will not be scheduling more until I finish the Sabbatical.

I am NOT shutting you down or out. I'm making a necessary decision that will essentially benefit all of us.

Let me also address the WHY, so there does not have to be any speculation. I've had some traumatic life, business and ministry experiences that I thought I'd work my way through and bounced back well. Today, during my session, I realized that I have not. There is more forgiveness needed. More healing needed. Deliverance is near! I don't believe the specifics of those traumas are necessary, however, I do know this new journey is.

So, with that said, I love you all and I'll be in touch soon!

Apostle J!

*****

I know you are probably thinking – wait! This lady is a Pastor? An Apostle? Yes! With churches, sons and daughters in ministry and all that? Yes! However, I intentionally left that out of the beginning of the story. It accurately represents how I wanted God to remove it from my life. After almost 20 years in ministry, 9 years total in pastoral roles, 4 years as a Senior Pastor, my prayer had become- God, I don't want to do *this* anymore. I wanted to act like it just didn't exist. I kept learning that I could not run or hide from any part of God's requirement and call on my life. Seemingly, not anywhere.

After feeling like it had all been in vain and that my dreams would never come true for so long, I wanted to silence the very existence of this part of my life. In my mind, if I could just be done with it or just go back to simply traveling and preaching, praying for people when needed then I'd be just fine. That was - "*in my mind.*" Clearly, it's not that simple. This thing is deeply rooted within me and it is... as the bible says – hope deferred had made my heart sick.

Did anyone know? Maybe, but not really. I'm sure some have tried to figure out how I was navigating what looked like failure. But there was no conversation about it. Did I share on this level? No! How could I? What was I supposed to say? And truthfully, it seemed that no one really cared enough to show up, support, or even ask.

I had more than enough shame and embarrassment. Truth is, I probably wouldn't have talked about it then anyway.

I've had more than enough of supporting other peoples' churches, ministry, and events without receiving the reciprocity of support from them.

Did I do it for that reason? No.

Did I think I would get it in return? Yes.

Why? My answer is why *not?* I always show up. I always sow. I'm always cheering others on. I roll up when people don't expect that I'm going to roll up. And it's genuine. So again, I ask- why not?

So, yes - I left that out. I started not to write about it at all. The truth is -some of my hardest, most traumatic disappointments, hurts and times of suffering in silence happened and stemmed from ministry and those I've supported in one way or another. I also know that some reading this will wonder how is that possible? Trust me, it is! I'm not the only one who has experienced it.

It's always the story that isn't told or seen by those looking in, that has caused so many of us to be in a place of silent suffering.

CHAPTER TWENTY- ONE

I had to be dreaming. I sat straight up in my bed. The room was dark except the sparks of light peeping through the blinds. I looked around for my phone, but it wasn't in the normal spot on my nightstand. I felt exhausted and slightly disoriented, so I leaned back on the large pillows I kept on my bed. I closed my eyes and did the breathing exercises that I'd taught others and that Dr. Corey recommended for me.

I shot up!

Dr. Corey! It did happen. Wait - the email! "Where's my phone? Did I really send that email out?"

I jumped off my bed frantically searching for my phone. "Jesus, why did I send that email? I could have kept going in ministry while I'm in this process. Lord, this is probably not going to go well. OMG! These people are going to wonder what kind of person they have been following in ministry. This isn't good. What was I thinking?" I was rushing around my room, talking to myself, frantically searching for my phone.

"Owwwwwwwwwwwwwwwww!!!!" I jumped and yelled!

I hit my left foot on the corner of the door leading to the hallway. I had to pause to let the pain semi-pass. It slowed me down, but I needed to get to my phone and fix this mess I'd made.

As I made my way down the stairs, albeit limping, I made it - I saw my peanut butter colored coach purse, car keys and Samsung S9 laying on the bottom step. I must have dropped them there when I came in. I grabbed the phone leaving everything else on the steps.

Immediately going to the Outlook application on my phone, I pulled up my email. I was going to retract it.

It was too late. Way too late!

Every last one of them had read it. And responded. I had 15 new email alerts. I wasn't ready to read them because I had no idea how they would respond.

I walked in the kitchen and laid the phone face down on the brown marble countertop. I wasn't ready yet. My mind started racing and thinking about how they had responded and what those emails might say. Leaning against the counter with my arms crossed over my chest, I closed my eyes and let out a deep breath. I just stood there with my thoughts.

The phone rang and jolted me out of them. "Oh no, I certainly don't want to talk right now." I looked at the phone with pure relief. It wasn't any of them. It was Dr. Corey. I answered immediately. I needed to tell her what I'd done.

"Dr. Corey. I'm glad it's you!" I know I must have sounded overly excited with my words rushing out.

"Well, I think that's a first." She chuckled. "I'm calling to follow up with you and see how you're doing this evening. Today was very intense and I know you may not have expected it to go as it did. How are you?"

"I don't know. The session was intense. I didn't expect that, but I did feel like I left the session better than when I came in. But now..." My words trailed off. I wasn't sure how to explain what I was feeling about the email.

"But now? What happened?" She patiently waited for me to get my words out.

"Well, I do feel like I left better than I came in. Apparently, I was so good, I sent an email to my leadership team and covenant ministry partners telling them I was taking Sabbatical. I actually told them that I am in therapy. I woke up from my nap and now I just don't think that was the best idea. I don't even know what made me want to share that. It's not like I can't do ministry and go through this process. I'm embarrassed. I went to retract the email and it was too late. It's too late. They've already read it. All of them. And responded. What am I supposed to do now?"

I said all that in one long unbroken breath, not necessarily for her to answer. I was really just spewing out my thoughts.

"What are you going to do about what?" She asked.

Exasperated, I answered her with rushed words again. "The email. I gave them too much information. I shouldn't have said I'm in therapy. How am I supposed to stand in front of them now?"

"Maiya!" Dr. Corey said sharply. I stilled myself for whatever she was about to say.

"Calm down." Her tone was much calmer and gentler now. "I called your name like that to snap you out of that frenzy. You don't have to do anything now. You didn't give them too much information. It's okay to share some parts, even vulnerable parts, with those you serve. Calm down, it's not going to be as bad as you think. You are most likely over thinking it."

"You sound so sure about that." That's the only response I could think of. My mind was still semi-racing. I wanted to believe what she said, but I knew how these things go when you're in ministry.

"How did they respond?"

"What?"

"How did they respond? What did they say? You said they all read it and responded."

"I don't know. I'm not ready to read the responses. There are literally 15 emails waiting for me, but I didn't open them. I can't.

"Oh, no ma'am! That is self-inflicted drama and what we are not going to do - is that. No ma'am! I'm glad I followed the unction of the Holy Spirit to call you at this moment. I was going to wait. Girl, if you don't go read those emails. You are most likely afraid of nothing."

"I'll read them later."

She laughed. "Girl, bye! Now, I know this is a new process to you but you're going to read those emails. Tonight. And call me in the morning so we can talk about it some more. I *will* be waiting. You can do this. And it won't be anything like you expect."

I sighed a deep sarcastic breath. "Okay." That was all I had.

"And one more thing, Maiya – just because you can do ministry and go through this process- doesn't mean you should."

I didn't respond. She was absolutely right. I would have told my people the same thing. As a matter of fact, I had told some of them this very thing. I had to eat my own words or as I say- take my own advice.

"Goodnight, Maiya. Talk to you in the morning."

"Goodnight."

CHAPTER TWENTY-TWO

"Lord, have mercy on me! This is crazy. I really have to calm down." I was thinking out loud when I got off the phone with Dr. Corey. I made some coffee and prepared myself to read the emails. I knew she would be waiting to hear from me just like she said.

I was headed back upstairs with my coffee and a blueberry muffin when my phone chimed. It was my armor bearer. I recognized her text tone. She was also my sister. I should have known she would be calling or texting if I had not responded to her email by now. If nobody else was going to reach out, she was going to. Period. She was the epitome of faithful, loyal and all out ride or die or as I called it - ride or fly.

I answered her text, but it was still quite a while before I read those emails.

I changed my mind about going back to bed. I turned and headed back downstairs to my home office. Sometimes, I would go in there just to sit and look out the window. One window in particular looked like what I described as a church window. If I wasn't mistaken, the wood trimming looked just like a cross. Sometimes, I'd just sit and look up. Other times, I'd pray and then sit and look up.

I walked into the space that was normally so calming for me and grabbed my favorite worn, tattered sweater. I brought it home with me from the office. It was something comforting about it, like an old friend. I wrapped it around myself as I stood in one of the other windows facing the back of the house. I just stood there. I thought about all the things that I needed to be doing, the book that I couldn't seem to finish, the other book I'd barely started. I thought about my ministries. My business. Tears welled up in my eyes. I drew the sweater tighter around me and let them fall.

I slowly paced the floor while tears seemed to fight to escape my eyes. Even crying alone was hard for me. I'd mastered holding it all in and keeping it moving.

I sat down in my favorite window seat and stretched my legs out. Hugging myself tight and taking multiple deep breaths, I was in such a broken place. A place that seemed more broken that I cared to admit or really knew how to express. The tears streamed uncontrollably, and it seemed that this semi-dark room was the only place I felt free enough to allow them to be released.

"Lord, am I in bondage to brokenness? I feel like there is literally no one that I can turn to. No one that I can call to talk to or pray for me. Who would I even trust my tears or my truth to? Wow! Lord, I feel so lost. Again. I'm hurting so much, God. The truth is I'm embarrassed. I'm ashamed. And I'm so hurt, God."

I was literally bent over as I silently cried out to God. Even after a few counseling sessions, finally releasing some things and crying out, there still seemed to be no real, lasting release. It seemed like I kept reverting back or at least going back and forth within myself.

I was in the house alone, nobody but God could hear me, but my cry was like a silent scream. My body sagged against the left side of the chair, my head seemed to drop further, my grip on myself seemed to loosen. I was alone.

"God, why am I a failure? I feel like everything I've done or ever started is a failure. I don't understand. How is this possible, God? Why did I start ministries that for so long, no one supported? Why am I good enough to be drained of everything I have in me but not good enough? Nothing really seems to be flourishing. Nothing. Everything You've assigned me to do has come with an insurmountable struggle. Even the conference - I continuously struggled to do it. Why, God? Am I doing what you want? Is this not what you told me to do? I did this at Your Word. I

don't want to give up…but I want to give up, Lord.

I wiped my face as I tried to catch my breath. By this point, I was sobbing. All I could get out were gut wrenching sobs. No words would come out. Embarrassment, shame, failure, and disappointment overwhelmed me. I was drowning.

I grabbed my pounding head in anguish. I tried to breathe through it. I couldn't. My thoughts started racing faster than I could keep up.

"God, please!" My heart screamed but my voice was swallowed up by uncontrollable sobs of distress. *"God, please."* I whispered.

I can't tell you how long the sobbing went on, only that it was painful. Physically, emotionally, mentally and spiritually. Finally, I had cried.

As the sobbing subsided, unending tears continued to stream down my face. I could feel them dropping on my hands and arms as I stilled myself. I sat quietly, rocking myself. It may have been minutes; it may have been hours. I honestly don't know.

I grabbed my turquoise blanket from the arm of the chair and pulled it over me. I wrapped myself up in it to combat the sudden chill I felt. I closed my eyes and simply was.

For the moment, I exhaled.

Sleep finally came.

CHAPTER TWENTY-THREE

It was hours later when I woke up. Looking up at my favorite window, I could see that it was still dark. I wasn't sure how long I'd slept. My mind still seemed foggy. I knew it was time to get up and face the music. I had put it off long enough, and I still didn't feel ready to look at those emails. I just knew that I had to.

"Gosh, I seem to be having a really hard time with this process, Lord. Why am I tripping like this? I'm no better than anyone else. This shouldn't be this hard for someone who advocates for others to receive therapy. I guess it really *is* different when the shoe is on the other foot."

I sighed heavily, shrugged my shoulders, and stood to fold up the blanket. I think I was just stalling. Finally, I headed up the stairs. It was now or never, and I was the one always teaching people not to procrastinate and face their fears. The emails were going to say what they were going to say whether I read them now or later.

As soon as I opened the first one, I gasped. I was immediately overwhelmed.

*****

From: The Boss!

To: The Covenant Crew

Re: Sabbatical

Thank you for doing what is needed for your healing and freedom. Thank you for not shutting down but giving us a glimpse of what has been going on in your life. Those truly in tune with God knew that there was something but weren't able to fully pinpoint what was going on.

Know that all things will be handled in excellence. You have taught us well. We are holding your arms up!

~ Boss!

*****

I opened the next one. I was speechless. Sometimes you really don't know what people will say or how they feel about you.

*****

From: Maria

To: The Covenant Crew

Re: Sabbatical

Wow! Wow! Wow! Now, I'm convinced! You're superwoman in disguise. I mean - Suffering in silence!!! Honestly Apostle, I'm amazed. We see you carrying on your day to day business, handling things in beast boss mode - we assumed you were alright! I'm so sorry that we missed this but so thankful that you're allowing us on the inside of what's going on with you.

I know from experience, that to finally be able to cut loose and talk about issues you once thought you had put to rest will breathe new life into you. YOU sent me to therapy! Listen, I can't speak for anybody else but I'm super proud of you! Ain't that deep!!! I'm proud of you lol.

The blessing is that this staff, the staff you trained - we got this! We are well equipped to handle the day to day workings of the ministry.

I decree that deliverance is coming! Not just for you but for us too! I already know when you come back it's going to be LIT!!! I love you dearly!

*****

From: Pastor Jen

To: The Covenant Crew

Re: Sabbatical

Apostle, may I have the name and number of the counseling center? If you can boldly and unashamedly expose yourself as you have, surely - I can follow your lead. You've encouraged me, numerous times, to go to therapy along with the sessions I've had with you. I hear you loud and clear. Your example is enough for me to know, it's my time. The problem with us as believers, especially leaders, is that we feel that once we get to a certain place, we are not supposed to hurt anymore, or at least not show it. Well, I'm hurting. You told me this over and over. Unfortunately, sometimes we feel that we are at an "I have arrived" place and things aren't going to affect us. I know this because I have been ashamed. I have a title, but I know how I've felt. Not knowing that it was ok. Okay to not be okay. I also know now, it's okay to get well. I'm going to counseling y'all! Thanks Mom!!

*****

"Jesus!" I couldn't speak in English for at least fifteen to twenty minutes. All I could do was worship God. That last email from Jen blew me away! I would have never thought that taking this step and sharing it would produce that! I always encouraged additional therapy, but I was simply knocked off my feet and wowed by God by that response. Who would have thought a decision to get well would release an anointing for others to follow suit!"

"God, You are a bad somebody!! You're good God! I mean real, real good!"

*****

Those emails went on and on and on. They were full of encouragement, hope and support. 15 emails later, not one negative word. And they started encouraging each other! I was overwhelmed with love and hope for myself. That was something I'd lost as well.

For so long, I was able to hope and believe for everyone else but not myself. Initially, I regretted sending that email but after spending two hours reading through the responses, shedding cleansing tears and finally responding to all of them, I felt a weight lift from my shoulders. I don't think I realized how much I was carrying until it shifted!

In that moment, God showed me success. What I viewed as failure because of the various times of struggle and disappointment - He allowed me to see that it was not. Through this outpour of love from these amazing Kingdom leaders, God showed me that He had allowed me to successfully build a team who functioned in love, unity, genuine support and led according to biblical standards.

"Well God, that's a win I will most certainly take. Thank You for proving me wrong once again. Thank You for showing me the power of what only You can do when I am submitted to You. I know You have them covered and I know they and the ministry will be okay while You and I work on me. Thank You, Lord.

Thank You for this love You've poured out on me even when I clearly didn't expect it. Thank You, thank You, thank You. You are a good God and I praise You! You are indeed my Father and I thank You! Thank You for letting me see that even this was orchestrated by You and what I saw as weakness, You can use that too. Oh yes God! This could only be You.

I ask You to make me better; I want to be complete and whole so that when You allow me to walk back in to serve them again, I can do so in a more excellent way! Glory to Your name, Father. Just glory!!"

As I prayed, I could sense the presence of God and it was so comforting. I felt a peace that I had not truly experienced in a very long time. It's amazing what love, support and honesty will do for you.

Once again, God shifted me and somehow, I knew brighter days were ahead.

CHAPTER TWENTY-FOUR

October 2, 2019

Journal Entry

It's been about three months since I started therapy and "the email."
The journey isn't over, but the process has helped me in so many ways.
Yesterday, I had a very enlightening session with Dr. Corey.

I'm even more grateful for the referral to the massage therapist. The
massages have been good for my physical body and my mind. The
young lady who owns Orchid Vitality in Buckhead, Dr. Yvette, is
simply amazing. Her knowledge, expertise and service have helped me
tremendously. I'm definitely going to refer everyone I know to her.

Since the passing of my dear friend, Dr. Martha, I had not had a
massage and didn't think I'd find anyone else. But the plan of God is so
specific and right for my life. Dr. Yvette is a breath of fresh air. Being
able to receive her services during this stressful and anxious time of life
has been comforting. I'm just amazed at how mindful of me that God
is.

Anyhoo, I've moved progressively forward in therapy and healing. I
feel like this night season is clearing up. I still have those stormy days,
but they aren't as dark as before and they haven't lasted as long. I don't
think I'm going back to work or ministry full time just yet, but I'm
finally able to hear and see a little clearer. I think it's time to have this
conference call with Melanie. I've postponed it long enough and now
that I'm better than I was, maybe I can help her.

*****

October 4, 2019

After I spent some time reviewing my notes from my last call with Melanie and praying, I was ready to call her again. The last call was a doozy. I remember it so well. Melanie was a wreck and truthfully, I was too. It was the day that I spontaneously decided to take leave. I don't know how God got me through that call with her but I'm grateful that He is always in control. That call could have gone many ways, but because of His grace toward both of us, I have an opportunity to come back to this matter and resolve it in His way, and timing.

*****

Conference Call Meeting with Melanie, Living With More Contracted Freelance Writer.

"Hi, Melanie. It's Maiya Jackson with Living With More Publications."

"Hi Maiya. I submitted my articles on time, is something wrong?" Her words rushed out anxiously.

"Not that I know of. I've been out of the office on medical leave, so I haven't seen your latest submissions. They've gone straight to your editor, Jonathan."

"Oh. I didn't realize you were out. I just thought that you assigned me to someone else because of our last conversation."

"I made the decision to take leave on the day that we spoke. It was not a result of our conversation, but it's been the best decision for me. The reason I'm calling today is to discuss your contract."

"Oh." She paused. "Can I ask you a question about that day?"

"Sure."

"What made you respond the way you did? You could have said anything, but you asked me could you pray for me? I still don't understand that."

"Oh, that's easy. God! As you were ranting and going IN and OFF may I add - God spoke to me. He would not allow me to respond like I could have or like I wanted to. Because of the Holy Spirit, I knew that what you needed was much more important than what I'd initially called for. So, I had to be obedient to God first and let everything else work itself out."

"Ohhhh. Wow!" She hurriedly spoke. "Please allow me to apologize for my attitude and harsh words during our last call. I was condescending; I spoke horribly to you and about your business. I was way out of line with my comments. The truth is - Your magazine is powerful and much different from any others I've read. I've actually been reading the full issues the last few months. I was, well – I am, in the middle of a divorce and I took my frustrations with this process and my hurt and anger out on you. I truly apologize for that. Instead of communicating, I allowed everything to fall apart."

"Well, I've been there before, and I understand how that can happen. Apology accepted. How are you now?

"I'm calmer but I'm still very distracted and trying to get my life together again. The divorce is close to being final, but the process is far from over."

"May I suggest something to you?"

"Sure."

"Try therapy."

"Oh no!" Melanie interjected, quickly cutting off my words. "I don't need *that*."

"Yes, you do. And as someone who has spent the last three months in formal therapy, I can attest - it works! You have to be open to it and honest with yourself. You need some help."

"I'm not crazy!" She almost yelled. "Why would I need to go talk to a shrink?"

I burst out laughing! Ha!

"Girl, please! I'm a business owner and let's not forget a whole minister of the Gospel and I needed H.E.L.P!

I'm not crazy either but the craziness of life sometimes requires us to seek out unbiased, medically trained help who can help us see clearer. And boo, you need some help! I encourage you to get over these stereotypes and think about how your life is about to shift once again. When this divorce is final, you're going to step into a whole new way of living, thinking, and being. And if your mind is not in a sound, stable place, it will be harder than it is now.

Going to therapy doesn't mean you're crazy. Going to therapy means you're taking responsibility for your mental health and your ability to live beyond the crazy in life. Going to therapy is going to help you navigate this new and different place in life with sound advice. It's a safe place to share those things you would otherwise hold in.

And take your children too! You are all going to need help! When you're ready, I can refer you to Grace Life Therapy. It *will* change your life."

Melanie chuckled slightly. "I can't believe you laughed. I honestly don't know what to say. But I'll think about it."

"Do that." "Now about this contract, let's talk."

We went through Melanie's contract line by line just as we did when she first signed. We resolved that December 2019 would be her last issue with us. For now.

Since we are moving into print, missed deadlines would be a hindrance to the growth and stability of the magazine.

Melanie and I agreed to revisit spotlight features once her life settled down, and she'd had time to readjust.

CHAPTER TWENTY-FIVE

November 1, 2019

Grace Life Therapy Group Therapy Session

"Okay, Lord. I'm going in this session and only You know if I'm really ready for this. When Dr. Corey talked to me about it, I immediately said no. But, here I am. I don't even know what I'm going to say, but, however you lead me, I'll follow."

I took a few deep breaths and exited my car. I was headed somewhere. Where - I wasn't sure, but I knew that I was better today than when I first walked into her office.

"Well good morning, Ms. Jackson. We are so excited that you are here! I can't wait to hear you speak!" The receptionist seemed to have a light shining within her. She was extremely excited.

"Good morning to you as well. I don't think I'm actually "speaking," however, I will share what God allows. I have a feeling it's going to be a different day."

"Oh yes ma'am, I think so too. I'll let Dr. Corey know you're here," she said as she hurried to the back. Today, Ms. Gloria seemed to move a little quicker and her eyes seemed to shine even brighter. Her joy encouraged me.

As I watched her hurry away, I realized that for the first time, I was comfortable in this room. I wasn't worried about being noticed or recognized. That was progress. I think I had gotten over myself. Finally.

*****

Group Session Room

When I walked in the room, there were loud gasps. It was loud. It came from several people in the room. More than one person in this room recognized me. I saw it on their faces. This time I didn't flinch. I didn't set my face like flint. I allowed it to be what it was. Whether they knew it or not, I was in the same place as them. Healing.

I prayed silently for myself and those in the room. *Alright Lord, here we go. This is all You. Help us all today, Holy Spirit.*

I took a seat quickly as Dr. Corey began her opening for the session.

"Good morning everyone! I'm so glad that you all agreed to this portion of your therapy journey. I believe today is going to be an exceptional, transforming day. We're going to address the elephant in the room so we can move past it," she chuckled.

"Many of you know and recognize Prophetess Chamaiya Jackson, world-renowned speaker and best-selling author. And we're certainly glad that she's here with us today. That's all I'll say about it for now. We'll let her share more before we end today."

Those in the room clapped and smiled as they looked toward me. I knew they were in for the shock of their life. I was just about sure that not many or any of them realized that I was a patient, not a guest. Although Dr. Corey asked me specifically to speak to this group, this was an assignment that was also *for* me.

"Alright everyone, let's chat," Dr. Corey said, drawing everybody's attention back in.

"I want to pose some questions to each of you to consider and you can choose to share or not. I realize some of you are not at that place yet, but for those who will, we'd love to hear from you."

The room was extremely quiet. Some appeared to be anxious. Some appeared to be present in body but not there mentally. I think I understood it all. Fortunately for me, I was fully present. That was another sign of growth and healing. I smiled.

Dr. Corey asked some simple but tough questions of the group. I didn't know which of them I wanted to or was prepared to answer. To everyone's surprise, once the first person started sharing, the others seemed to open up. The group discussion became very lively.

There were more gasps and wide-eyed looks as people shared bits of their stories. There was laughter as others shared how Dr. Corey quickly got them together in one or more of their sessions. I didn't share much about my sessions because I hadn't revealed nor had Dr. Corey that I was a patient as well. I did share some of my *Life's Experiences* though. Some of them had read my story in my book, *Hurt to Healing*. I was able to share with them how God gave me different *Articles of Encouragement* during some very rough times, and how I used those *Meditations* to help and heal my heart, mind and soul.

That blond haired, five feet tall woman had such a tall job that she was obviously doing well. Her fruit was right there in that room.

"Okay everyone, it's been an amazing session. I must say that I'm shocked at all of you. I mean that in a very good way. The progress that you've all made makes my labor more than worth it. I'm so glad about what has taken place here today.

Now, the moment I know many of you are waiting for; Prophetess Jackson is going to close out our meeting today. Let's receive her."

They started clapping again. I was slightly embarrassed. I wondered if they would still be clapping once they realized that I was actually a patient. Either way, it was time.

I took a few deep breaths, squared my shoulders and addressed the group, stepping back into what I was called to do in a much different and better place.

CHAPTER TWENTY- SIX

"Good afternoon, everyone. It's been an amazing morning. Thank you for your warm reception. Let's thank God for this amazing vessel and therapist that we have in Dr. Corey."

Another round of applause sprang up in the room. A couple of hallelujahs and thank ya's could be heard as well.

"Y'all, we're so churchy," I laughed. We all laughed.

"I'm very grateful to be here with each of you today. You have some amazing stories and you've overcome so much! I was almost overwhelmed listening to your highs and lows; your challenges and triumphs. What I love most is that each of you overcame *you and* made the necessary decision to enter this life changing process of therapy and healing at Grace Life.

I've had to overcome *me* as well in many ways, as you have. I've had highs and lows, oh - the lows! I've had challenges and triumphs like yours. Sitting in this room is such a sweet reminder that we are not alone. We are not the only one experiencing what we've lived through. God has so much for our lives if we'd grab hold of it.

"I believe that many of you started grabbing hold of what God has for you when you entered the doors of Grace Life and submitted to the help you needed."

I paused and took a long, deep breath. "So did I."

I paused again; this time a little longer...so my words could sink in.

Some understood immediately. Their wide-eyed shocked looks told me so. Some of them still didn't fully grasp what I was sharing.

"I had to overcome me. Actually - I had to get over myself. It was way past time for me to acknowledge the hurt, the pain, the place that I was **stuck** in, and enter into the help that I needed."

This time, I put strong emphasis on **"I."**

"That help was here. And today, you've added to my help. I can see how easy it may have been to think, oh - she's here to empower and encourage us because of who God has called me to be. While it's true that I am here to share with you - not in the way that you think.

Today, instead of being a guest - I *am* you. You *are* me. *We* are products of Grace Life Therapy. Today, I'm more honored to be a thriving patient than a guest speaker. Just as you came in those doors and had a hard time releasing things and other things were a bit easier – me too! Just as you needed this place of power and peace and safety – so did I. Just as you said Dr. Corey shut you down in good fashion – whew, me too!"

There was a loud burst of laughter all over the room. I had connected with them.

"Let me share my shut down story! I think my shut down trumps all of yours! She was brutal!"

More laughter rang out in the room. As I shared the details of the day that I was ready to turn tail and run out of the room, smiles could be seen, and the laughter got louder. Even I was laughing at this point. It was a gut hugging, tears in my eye's kind of laughter, and oh my goodness - how good it felt. And this time, I didn't stop myself.

"Whew!" I found myself laughing at myself and feeling freer than ever. At some point, somehow, my arms shot up in a full wave! I felt the presence of God. My laughter seemed more like worship as I embraced this place that God had brought me to.

I made it through that moment of unashamedly revealing myself to people who could have shunned me, or rejected ministry from me, because I had an issue. Instead, there was acceptance, realization that no one has it all together no matter how put together they seem, and there was encouragement. Once I got over myself again in that moment, I was able to fully step into the other reason Dr. Corey invited me to the group. In her words, "this group needs the oil of God's anointing that's on your life. You're in a better place spiritually and clinically. It's time for you to step back in."

Beyond the laughter, which did turn into a full-blown time of intimate worship right there in the therapy room, God began to speak through me. There were many prophetic words released and God was glorified. That was yet another divine setup by God – for me. I needed that safe space to prophesy and flow in the oil and power of God. Who knew therapy would open such a door for me? More importantly, for God?

Hear me good, this wasn't about ministering as much as it was about receiving ministry. Yes, this would definitely become a part of my ministry. As I continue to heal and grow, I'll help others on a greater level. However, the freedom to be me, unashamed, not embarrassed, with no mask, was what ministered to me that day.

Now, I could sing my single *"I'm Free"* and it be totally true!

I am no longer bound, no longer chained, no longer down. I'm Free! I'm free to be me!

Is my healing journey over? No. Not by any means. This was truly just the beginning!

CHAPTER TWENTY- SEVEN

December 2019

The drive into the office was wonderful. It's the holiday season and traffic was a little lighter than usual. It's the last day before the staff takes off to enjoy friends and family.

Angie organized the annual Christmas luncheon specifically for the day that I was returning. I arrived early and parked on the furthest end of the parking lot. No one knew I was coming today except Angie. I couldn't wait to see my staff, love on them and release some well-earned bonuses to them. I also couldn't wait to thank them. Their love, support, calls, texts, emails, continued hard work, and the meals during my time off, was very refreshing. They helped me to heal in many ways.

Entering the building, I breathed deep, as I slowly walked the halls of my beloved company. I smiled as I passed each conference room, the staff breakroom, greeted the security guards as they were changing shifts, and made my way upstairs to my office. I was grateful.

For a while, I thought that we would not survive. Sales were not always what we needed or projected them to be. Contractors didn't always meet their deadlines and threw us, mainly Jonathan, into a tailspin. But God is good! Payroll was always met. We didn't have to downsize. And although some major changes are on the horizon, Living With More will make it.

I'm also full of gratitude because I was able to take the time I needed. I did so without fear of what might or might not happen. As their CEO, I had the opportunity to become better for them, the business, and our clients.

Speaking of clients, I did do a little work while I was out. That's the other reason I was back today. I would be announcing the launching of our new Publishing Department. While I was out, I signed seven new authors who are ready to roll out their books. As a best-selling author and after years of publishing my own books, being mentored by the one and only Suprina Frazier, International Best-Selling Author and Fan Favorite, I was well equipped to equip others. I was armed with knowledge, information, revelation and experience that would help shape the visions of other rising authors.

I would also be announcing the launch of our Layout Design Department. Yes, we already had a department that did this for our magazine. Moving forward, we'd be offering our design services to other indie magazine owners. There is more than enough room for all of us in this big ole' world. My goal is to help others as I am being helped.

The best news is that this would mean there would be some in house promotions and increases. Others would be given the opportunity to grow and learn in new areas. We weren't downsizing. We're expanding!

I sat in my office, smiling, teary eyed because of the grace of God and His amazing goodness. When I thought I was going to lose it all, He turned it around for the good of everyone. That turn-around - started with me.

CHAPTER TWENTY-EIGHT

Tapping the microphone, Angie opened up our celebration. "Well team, it's been a super amazing year," she said.

She was standing at the front of the huge meeting room that had been transformed into a holiday-a-rama. That girl loved Christmas. Every year, she went above and beyond to make this time so special for the staff. This year, it seemed that she'd pour her heart and soul into this.

I stood in the small meeting room to the left listening as she talked about their amazing contributions and accomplishments. Name after name was called, awards were given out, loud applause could be heard with each one. There was plenty of laughter and food to go around.

As Angie finished up the awards, she announced that a surprise speaker would be joining them shortly. She also mentioned that some major announcements would be shared before they left.

"Alright, everyone. Congratulations to you all. Each of you are deserving of these honors and Living With More is extremely blessed to have you on our team."

There was applause but there were also whispers as they tried to figure out who this surprise speaker was. What they wanted to know even more, was what were the major announcements.

"I'm not going to keep you all in suspense any longer. I see your minds working already so I'm pleased to tell you that our surprise speaker for today is…"

Before she said my name, I opened the meeting room door. To my complete surprise, the room exploded.

"Yooooooo, It's Ms. J!!!!"

"Ms. J.!!!"

"Mama J!!!"

"Yesssssssssssssssssssssssssssssssss, she's here!!!!"

"Maiya!!!!"

All I remember hearing was my name being yelled in several different ways and loud claps. Before I knew it, the whole room bombarded me. I couldn't even step into the door good.

Oh, my goodness, what an amazing feeling. It felt like love. I couldn't hug everyone fast enough. I couldn't believe there were tears in this room and all of this hoopla. My mouth was literally hanging open. Needless to say, I was not expecting quite that reaction. But I'll be honest, it was such a welcomed and blessed reception. This moment taught me that often, there are more people for you, who love you sincerely and are rooting for you more than you know.

Once the room calmed down and the tears subsided some, I was able to speak to them from my heart.

"My goodness! I didn't expect that at all but thank you. I feel so loved right now, and that love is reciprocated. I'm so grateful for each of you. As I listened to Angie call out names and awards from next door, I couldn't help but feel so proud and honored to know each of you. I couldn't let the year end without being back here with you.

Thank you! Thank you! Thank you!

Your dedication, hard work and consistency makes this company everything that it is. The grace that's on your life to do what you do and to do it so well is a blessing to Living With More and to me.

"And Angie! Y'all give it up for my sister, my friend, my partner. You are one in a million. Without you, I would not have made it. Thank you for hanging in here with me. Thank you for understanding. Thank you for staying the course even when you didn't understand. Thank you for stepping in and running my vision as if it's your own and never making me feel like it was too much.

All of you - I value the work that you do but above that, I value *you*. Every one of you. Not one of you is less important than the other. Because of you, I was able to step away and get better. And I am better."

I shared some of my therapy journey with them and made them laugh about how I wanted to run away from therapy, but I'd met my match in the fiery Dr. Corey. I encouraged those who had opted to begin therapy at Grace Life to continue the journey. I encouraged those who were still on the fence about it to decide to live and be better. Grace Life could help them do both. I was living proof.

"I have one last announcement before we party on, and then go be with our families for the holidays."

The room grew quiet quickly. They almost looked a little nervous, but after the promotion announcements, I thought it was time to give out the bonuses.

"This year, your work has helped us to increase sales, our marketing solutions have proven to work better than we expected, and you have shown downright commitment and loyalty to this company. Because of you, we are able to give you each an additional $750 bonus. This is on top of the bonus you've already received."

"Yesssssssssssssss!!!"

"This is why we love LWM!"

"Come on God!!"

"Thank you, Jesus!"

"Won't He do it!!"

That was just a little bit of what was heard resounding in the room. I saw some tears too, which let me know - God had just come through for some people.

"And on that note, have a great Christmas and New Year. I'll see you all in January."

"Wait! What?" Jonathan bucked his eyes and his arms were just about to start flaying.

"Jonathan! It is well. It's taken care of. You all deserve these two weeks off. With pay."

Thunderous claps and loud thank you's took over the room! It was such a blessing to be able to bless them after all they'd done for me and my company.

We spent the next hour laughing, eating and fellowshipping.

I was glad to be back.

I was glad to still be here.

I was glad to be better.

CHAPTER TWENTY- NINE

Intentionally being late for worship services was not what I normally did, but today was different. I was about to step back into a community that I'd labored with and loved so deeply. I didn't want to distract them with my presence. It had been months since many of them had seen me. We'd talked and chatted via text, but I had not worshipped with them. I visited other churches where I felt I could blend in, not be seen, and simply be in the presence of God. But it was time to come out of hiding now.

How I missed the sound of worship at Destiny Worship Center International! There was no sound quite like that of our amazing Worship Pastor, Prophetess Jen! Thankfully, I didn't have to miss out on this part too much. For the last few months, she sent me video clips daily, of her morning devotion as she sang unto the Lord. Those few minutes of worship in song were sometimes just enough to get me up out the bed some days. It was good to be back for the full experience though. At the moment, it sounded like she was giving it everything she had.

I checked myself once more in the wall length mirror in my office and steadied myself to embrace this well missed place once again.

"I guess it's time for me to make this re-entrance."

I loved my church, even with all of the challenges we've had over the years. I learned that much of it came with the territory. I'd also resolved that while my journey had sometimes been tumultuous and other times more than a challenge, the joy that I experienced in my assignment is unmatched.

I made my way to the side entrance of the sanctuary where I would normally enter. I stood at the door listening to the sounds of worship; the fully engaged congregation was such a beautiful sight. It was always a blessing when people could be fully engaged with God in worship without phones, recording devices and other distractions.

When it was time for the opening scripture to prepare for the message, I stepped inside the door- making my way quickly to the seat on the end of the first row. That is right. I did NOT take the pulpit, go for the microphone nor was I preaching today. I'm back, but I'm here to receive from these vessels that have been carrying this ministry in a most effective way while I was on sabbatical.

This was the perfect time to return. It was what most people called "homecoming." All of the Pastors of Destiny Worship Center International, from different campuses, brought all of their teams and partners. Today, they would all be sharing brief messages with us. I'm super excited about how God orchestrated this day.

****

At the end of service, I addressed the congregation briefly. I thanked them for their love, support and continued dedication to the work God is doing through Destiny Worship Centers around the Nation.

"Destiny Seekers!!!!" Yep, I was shouting. "It is so good to be back with you today. It's good to be back and to be better. These last few months have been transformative for me and over the next few weeks and months, I will openly share with you why my therapy treatments were necessary and remain an important part of my life.

I wanted to take a brief moment to say, thank you for loving me, thank you for remaining steadfast, and thank you for continuing to walk with me and the leaders of DWCI as we follow Christ, our leader. I love you all tremendously. I'm looking forward to where God will lead us and the transformation that's about to hit this house! God sent me out to become better, so that all of us can become better. Stay tuned to God. Something amazing is about to happen!"

Loud praise, several hallelujah's and other sentiments of praise and worship rang out in the sanctuary. I left the pulpit to have a quick meeting with my leaders then on to fellowship with the beautiful people of our ministry. It was good to be among them, to hear the words of encouragement from some of them and to feel that genuine love that we always tried to share with every person we encountered.

I was also wonderfully surprised to find out that Layla, the young waitress at Bre's, had become an active member of our ministry. As much as we'd communicated over the previous months, I was surprised she kept this secret. She told me about her promotion to Shift Manager at Bre's, updated me on the kids and her college enrollment, but this one - she held out on me. Nevertheless, I was ecstatic to see her. We spoke briefly and she promised to bring me up to speed with this amazing news and how it came to be.

What most people don't know is that for as many people as I pour into, rarely do I invite them to become members of our church. My invitation is always to Christ. My advice is always to find a Bible teaching church that applies what they teach and become more rooted and grounded in the Word of God. It's always an added blessing when they decide to join us in worship.

Of course, Bre' was there. She knew I'd be returning today. Our relationship was even closer since I started out on this healing journey. We'd talked just about every day while I was gone. She had been an active member of DWCI since its' inception. What I appreciated most was that she didn't feel the need to tell me every little thing that happened while I was away. She trusted those in leadership and supported them just as she supported me. That meant so much to me.

I was also super excited to see her today, because it was the opening of the "mini" Bre's inside our church. The cafe would be open anytime the church was open, offering food and beverage services to the members and visitors. She would also serve as the official ministry culinary leader. This café was a dream come true for me. I was so glad that Bre' was a part of this dream being fulfilled. Little did I know that Latrell, who had graduated college earlier this year, would be the manager for our location.

Expansion was happening all around us and I was extremely glad to be alive to experience it. I'm grateful to be able to be present in the moment, with a sound, clear mind. I guess I could say that overall, today was a good day.

Morning had finally come…It turned out that what I'd heard, was true for me too.

The Healing Journey Continues….

FINAL WORDS
From My Heart to Yours

This was not just another story. It's a true one. While I weaved in story details for your reading pleasure, most of what you read is my real-life journey. Too often, many people are suffering in silence while serving. I've decided to break the silence and put an end to the silent suffering. I'm called to serve, and although there is a level of suffering that comes with the assignment, I'm navigating the call and its requirements differently and better.

If you have been suffering in silence and haven't taken time to pull away and take care of yourself, specifically your mental health, I strongly encourage you to do so. As I said in the book, therapy doesn't mean you're crazy. Going to therapy means you're taking responsibility for your mental health and your ability to live beyond the craziness of life. Going to therapy is going to help you navigate new, different and difficult places in life with sound advice and a safe place to share those things you would otherwise hold in.

Don't allow stigmas and lack of knowledge to keep you away from your healing and wholeness. Mental health is just as important as your physical health. In fact, I've come to believe that our mental health severely impacts our physical health, both negatively and positively.

I leave you with these two scriptures as you consider the things you may be experiencing and your own need to pull away and seek help:

Psalm 30:5 NKJV- For His anger is but for a moment, His favor is for life; **Weeping may endure for a night, But joy comes in the morning.**

3 John 1:2 **NKJV- Beloved, I pray that you may prosper in all things and be in health, just as your soul prospers.**

Get Well Soon!

LaTrice Williams, The Destiny Driver

ABOUT THE AUTHOR

LaTrice Williams, The Destiny Driver, is God's servant, first and foremost. A child of the King, she is a Servant Leader, Senior Pastor & Founder of Divine Grace Ministries Int'l. She is the CEO and founder of *LaTrice Williams Ministries* and *Living With More.* In addition to *Such a Long Night,* she is also the best-selling author of *Hurt to Healing, Articles of Encouragement,* and *Meditations- Heart, Mind & Soul.* She is also the author of *Life's Experience,* her first book penned in 2004. In 2018, she created The *Destiny Journal.*

As an ordained minister of the Gospel, *LaTrice* enjoys sharing the Word of God through many avenues. She will literally preach and teach her shoes off as she endeavors to empower, encourage and strengthen others to pursue their passion, live in wholeness and receive the healing that is available for their lives. She enjoys training and equipping future leaders for the Kingdom.

LaTrice is living to serve God through serving HIS people in love and in excellence. With the hand of the Lord on her and the ministries He has called her to, she will live out her God-ordained purpose in the earth.

www.ingramcontent.com/pod-product-compliance
Lightning Source LLC
Chambersburg PA
CBHW071136250626
47159CB00006B/2235